About Liz Fielding

Liz Fielding was born with itchy feet. She made it to Zambia before her twenty-first birthday and, gathering her own special hero and a couple of children on the way, lived in Botswana, Kenya and Bahrain—with pauses for sightseeing pretty much everywhere in between. She finally came to a full stop in a tiny Welsh village cradled by misty hills, and these days mostly leaves her pen to do the travelling.

When she's not sorting out the lives and loves of her characters, she potters in the garden, reads her favourite authors and spends a lot of time wondering, *What if...?*

For news of upcoming books—and to sign up for her occasional newsletter—visit Liz's website: **www.lizfielding.com**

Anything But Vanilla...

Liz Fielding

MILLS & BOON

First published in Great Britain 2013
by Mills & Boon, an imprint of Harlequin (UK) Limited.
Harlequin (UK) Limited, Eton House, 18-24 Paradise Road,
Richmond, Surrey TW9 1SR

© Liz Fielding 2013

ISBN: 978 0 263 23477

Harlequin (UK) policy
and recyclable products
forests. The logging and manufacturing process conform to the
legal environmental regulations of the country of origin.

Printed and bound in Great Britain
by CPI Antony Rowe, Chippenham, Wiltshire

Also by Liz Fielding

The Last Woman He'd Ever Date
Flirting With Italian
Tempted by Trouble
Mistletoe and the Lost Stiletto
SOS: Convenient Husband Required
A Wedding at Leopard Tree Lodge
Her Desert Dream
Secret Baby, Surprise Parents
Wedded in a Whirlwind

Did you know these are also available as eBooks?
Visit www.millsandboon.co.uk

TM

This book is dedicated to the authors
with whom I share my writing life.
They are my support group, a cyber hug away when
the writing is tough and, when life gives you lemons,
they're always on hand to make lemonade.

CHAPTER ONE

There's nothing more cheering than a good friend when we're in trouble—except a good friend with ice cream.
—*from Rosie's 'Little Book of Ice Cream'*

'Hello? Shop?'

Alexander West ignored the rapping on the shop door, the call for attention. The closed sign was up; Knickerbocker Gloria was out of business. End of story.

The accounts were a mess, the petty cash tin contained nothing but paper clips and he'd found a pile of unopened bills in the bottom drawer of the desk. All the classic signs of a small business going down the pan and Ria, with her fingers in her ears, singing la-la-la as the creditors closed in.

It was probably one of them at the door now. Some poor woman whose own cash flow was about to hit the skids hoping to catch her with some loose change in the till, which was why this wouldn't wait.

He topped up his mug with coffee, eased the ache in his shoulder and set about dealing with the pile of unopened bills.

There was no point in getting mad at Ria. This was his fault.

She'd promised him that she'd be more organised, not let things get out of hand. He was so sure that she'd learned her lesson, but maybe he'd just allowed himself to be convinced simply because he wanted it to be true.

She tried, he knew she did, and everything would be fine for a while, but then she'd hear something, see something and it would trigger her depression…get her hopes up. Then, when they were dashed, she'd be ignoring everything, especially the scary brown envelopes. It didn't take long for a business to go off the rails.

'Ria?'

He frowned. It was the same voice, but whoever it belonged to was no longer outside—

'I've come to pick up the Jefferson order,' she called out. 'Don't disturb yourself if you're busy. I can find it.'

—but inside, and helping herself to the stock.

He hauled himself out of the chair, took a short cut across the preparation room—scrubbed, gleaming and ready for a new day that was never going to come—and pushed open the door to the stockroom.

All he could see of the 'voice' was a pair of long, satin-smooth legs and a short skirt that rode up her thighs and stretched across a neat handful of backside. It was an unexpected pleasure in what was a very bad day and, in no hurry to halt her raid on the freezer, he leaned against the door making the most of the view.

She muttered something and reached further into its depths, balancing on one toe while extending the other towards him as if inviting him to admire the black suede shoe clinging to a long, slender foot. A high-heeled black suede shoe, cut away at the side and with a saucy bow on the toe. Very expensive, very sexy and designed to display a foot, an ankle, to perfection. He dutifully admired the ankle, the leg, a teasing glimpse of lace—that skirt was criminally short—and several inches of bare flesh where her top had slithered forward, at his leisure.

The combination of long legs and dark red skirt, sandwiched between cream silk and lace, reminded him of a cone filled with Ria's home-made raspberry ripple ice cream. It had been a while since he'd been within touching distance of temptation but now, recalling that perfect mix of fresh tangy fruit and creamy sweetness, he contemplated the idea of scooping her up and running his tongue along the narrow gap of golden skin at her waist.

'I've got the strawberry and cream gelato and the cupcakes, Ria.' Her voice, sexily breathless as she shifted containers, echoed from the depths of the freezer. 'And I've found the bread and honey ice cream. But there's no Earl Grey granita, champagne sorbet or cucumber ice cream.'

Cucumber ice cream?

No wonder Ria was in trouble.

He took a final, appreciative look at the endless legs and, calling the hormones to heel, said, 'If it's not there, then I'm sorry, you're out of luck.'

Sorrel Amery froze.

Metaphorically as well as literally. With her head deep in the freezer and nothing but a strappy silk camisole between her and frozen to death, she was already feeling the chill, but either Ria had the worst sore throat in history, or that was—

She hauled herself out of its chilly depths and turned round.

—not Ria.

She instinctively ran her hands down the back of a skirt that her younger sister—with no appreciation of vintage fashion—had disparagingly dismissed as little more than a pelmet. It was, however, too late for modesty and on the point of demanding who the hell the man leaning against the prep-room door thought he was, she decided against it.

Silence was, according to some old Greek, a woman's best garment and, while it was not a notion she would generally subscribe to, hot blue eyes above a grin so wide that it would struggle to make it through the door were evidence enough that he'd been filling his boots with the view.

Whoever he was, she wasn't about to make his day by going all girly about it.

'Out of luck? What do mean, out of luck?' she demanded. 'Where's Ria?' Brisk and businesslike were her first line of defence in the face of a sexy male who thought all he had to do was smile and she'd be putty in his hands.

So wrong—although the hand propping him up against the door frame had a workmanlike appearance: strong, broad and with deliciously long fingers that looked as if they'd know exactly what to do with putty...

She shivered a little and the grin twitched at the corner of his mouth, suggesting that he knew exactly what she was thinking.

Wrong again.

She was just cold. *Really.* She hadn't stopped to put on the cute, boxy little jacket that completed her ensemble. This wasn't a business meeting, but a quick in-and-out pick-up of stock.

While the jacket wouldn't have done anything for her legs, it would have covered her shoulders and kept her warm. And when she was wearing a suit, no matter how short the skirt, she felt in control. Important when you were young and female and battling to be taken seriously in a world that was, mostly, dominated by men.

In suits.

But she didn't have to impress Ria and hadn't anticipated the freezer diving. Or the audience.

The man lounging against the door frame clearly didn't feel the need for armour of any kind, beyond the heavy stubble on his chin and thick brown hair that brushed his shoulders and flopped untidily around his face.

No suit for him. No jacket. Just a washed-out T-shirt stretched across wide shoulders, and a pair of shabby jeans moulded over powerful thighs. The sun streaks that brightened his hair—and the kind of skin-deep tan that you didn't get from two weeks on a beach—only confirmed the impression that he didn't believe in wasting his time slaving over a hot desk, although the suggestion of bags under his eyes did suggest a heavy night-life.

'Ria's not here.' His voice, low and gravelly, lazy as his stance, vibrated softly against her breastbone, as if he'd reached out and grazed his knuckles slowly along its length. It stole her breath, circling softly before settling low in her belly and draining the strength from her legs. 'I'm taking care of things.'

She fumbled for the edge of the freezer, grasping it for support. 'Oh? And you are?' she asked, going for her 'woman in command of her environment' voice and falling miserably short. Fortunately, he didn't know that. As far as he knew, she always talked in that weirdly breathy way.

'Alexander West.'

She blinked. 'You're the postcard man?'

'The what?' It was his turn to look confused, although, since he was already leaning against the door, he didn't need propping up.

'The postcard man,' she repeated, desperately wishing she'd kept her mouth shut, but the nickname had been startled out of her. For one thing he was younger than she'd expected. Really. Quite a lot younger. Ria wore her age well, but wasn't coy about it, describing her fortieth birthday as a moment of 'corset-loosening' liberation. Not that she'd ever needed a corset, or would have worn one if she had. 'That's what Nancy calls you,' she explained, in an attempt to distance herself from her surprised reaction. 'Ria's assistant? You send her postcards.'

'I send postcards to Nancy?' he asked, the teasing gleam in his eyes suggesting that he was perfectly aware of her discomfort and the reason for it.

'To Ria. Very occasionally,' she added. Having regained a modicum of control over her vocal cords, if nothing else, she wanted him to know that she wasn't impressed by him or his teasing.

It wasn't the frequency of their arrival that made the post-cards memorable, but their effect. She'd once found Ria clutching one to her breast, tears running down her cheeks. She'd waved away her concern, claiming that it was hay fever. In November.

Only a lover, or a child, could evoke that kind of response. Alexander West was a lot younger than she'd expected, but he wasn't young enough to be her son, which left only one possibility, although in this instance it was a lover who was notable only by his absence. His cards, when they did arrive, were mostly of long white tropical beaches fringed with palm trees. The kind that evoked Hollywood-style dreams of exotic cocktails and barefoot walks along the edge of the shore with someone who looked just like Mr Postcard. Sitting at home in Maybridge, it was scarcely any wonder Ria was weeping.

'Once in a blue moon,' she added, in case he hadn't got the message.

Sorrel knew all about the kind of travelling man who took advantage of a warm-hearted woman before moving on, leaving her to pick up the pieces and carry on with her life. Her own father had been that kind of man, although he had never bothered with even the most occasional postcard. Forget moons—blue or any other colour—his visit was on the astronomical scale of Halley's Comet. Once in a lifetime.

'A little more frequently than that, I believe,' he replied. 'Or were you using the term as a figure of speech rather than an astronomical event?' Fortunately, the question was rhetorical because, without waiting for an answer, he added, 'I'm not often in the vicinity of a post office.'

'You don't have to explain yourself to me,' she said, making an effort to get a grip, put some stiffeners in her knees.

Not at all.

'I'm glad to hear it.' West let go of the door and every cell in her body gave a little jump—of nervousness, excitement, anticipation—but he was only settling himself more comfortably, leaning his shoulder against the frame, crossing strong, sinewy arms and putting a dangerous strain on the stitches holding his T-shirt together. 'I thought perhaps you were attempting to make a point of some kind.'

'What?' Sorrel realised that she was holding her breath... 'No,' she said, unable to look away as one of the stitches popped, then another, and the seam parted to reveal a glimpse of the golden flesh beneath. She swallowed. Hard. 'The frequency of your correspondence is none of my business.'

'I know that, but I was beginning to wonder if *you* did.' The gleam intensified and without warning she was feeling anything but cold. Her head might be saying, 'He is so not your type...' She did not do lust at first sight.

Her body wasn't listening.

It had tuned out her brain and was reaching out to him with fluttery little 'touch me' appeals from her pulse points, the tight betraying peaks of her breasts poking against the thin silk...

No, no, no, no, no!

She swallowed, straightened her spine, hoping that he'd put that down to the cold air swirling up from the open freezer. She continued to cling to it, not for support, but to stop herself from taking a step closer. Flinging herself at him. That was what her mother, who'd made a life's work of lust at first sight and had three fatherless daughters to show for it, would have done.

Since the age of seventeen, when that legacy had come back to bite her and break her teenage heart, she had made a point of doing the opposite of whatever her mother would do in any circumstance that involved a man. Especially avoiding the kind of rough-hewn men who, it seemed, could turn her head with a glance.

Sorrel had no idea what had brought Alexander West back to Maybridge, but from her own reaction it was obvious that his arrival was going to send Ria into a meltdown tizzy. Worse, it would cause no end of havoc to the running of Knickerbocker Gloria, which was balanced on the edge of chaos at the best of times. The knock-on effect was going to be the disruption of the business she was working so hard to turn into a high-end event brand.

Presumably Ria's absence this morning meant that she was having a long lie-in to recover from the enthusiastic welcome home she'd given the prodigal on his return.

He looked pretty shattered, too, come to think of it...

Sorrel slammed the door shut on the images that thought evoked. It was going to take a lot more than a pair of wide, here-today-gone-tomorrow shoulders to impress her.

Oh, yes.

While her friends had been dating, she'd had an early reality check on the value of romance and had focused on her future, choosing the prosaic Business Management degree and vowing that she'd be a millionaire by the time she was twenty-five.

Any man who wanted her attention would have to match her in drive and ambition. He would also have to be well groomed, well dressed, focused on his career and, most important of all, stationary.

The first two could be fixed. The third would, inevitably, be a work in progress, but her entire life had been dominated by men who caused havoc when they were around and then disappeared leaving the women to pick up the pieces. The last was non-negotiable.

Alexander West struck out on every single point, she told

herself as another stitch surrendered, producing a flutter of excitement just below her waist. Anticipation. Dangerous feelings that, before she knew it, could run out of control and wreck her lifeplan, no matter how firmly nailed down.

'What, exactly, are you doing here?' she demanded. If the cold air swirling around at her back wasn't enough to cool her down, all she had to do was remind herself that he belonged to Ria.

She was doing a pretty good job of cool and controlled, at least on the surface. Having faced down sceptical bank managers, sceptical marketing men and sceptical events organisers, she'd had plenty of practice keeping the surface calm even when her insides were churning. Right now hers felt as if a cloud of butterflies had moved in.

'That's none of your business, either.'

'Actually, it is. Ria supplies me with ice cream for my business and since she has apparently left you in charge for the day...' major stress on 'apparently' '...you should be aware that, while you are in a food-preparation area, you are required to wear a hat,' she continued, in an attempt to crush both him and the disturbing effect he and his worn-out seams were having on her concentration. 'And a white coat.'

A white coat would cover those shoulders and thighs and then she would be able to think straight.

'Since Knickerbocker Gloria is no longer in business,' he replied, 'that's not an issue.' Had he placed the slightest emphasis on *knicker*? He nodded in the direction of the cartons she had piled up on the table beside the freezer and said, 'If you'll be good enough to return the stock to the freezer, I'll see you off the premises.'

It took a moment for his words to filter through.

'Stock? *No longer in...* What on earth are you talking about? Ria knows I'm picking up this order today. When will she be here?'

'She won't.'

'Excuse me?' She understood the words, but they were spinning around in her brain and wouldn't line up. 'Won't what?'

'Be here. Any time soon.' He shrugged, then, taking pity on her obvious confusion—he was probably used to women losing the power of speech when he flexed his biceps—he said, 'She had an unscheduled visit from the Revenue last week. It seems that she hasn't been paying her VAT. Worse, she's been ignoring their letters on the subject and you know how touchy they get about things like that.'

'Not from personal experience,' she replied, shocked to her backbone. Her books were updated on a daily basis, her sales tax paid quarterly by direct debit. Her family had lived on the breadline for a very long time after one particularly beguiling here-today-gone-tomorrow man had left her family penniless.

She was never going back there.

Ever.

There was nothing wrong with her imagination, however. She knew that 'touchy' was an understatement on the epic scale. 'What happened? Exactly,' she added.

'I couldn't say, exactly. Using my imagination to fill the gaps I'd say that they arrived unannounced to carry out an audit, took one look at her books and issued her with an insolvency notice,' he said, without any discernible emotion.

'But that means—'

'That means that nothing can leave the premises until an inventory has been made of the business assets and the debts paid or, alternatively, she's been declared bankrupt and her creditors have filed their claims.'

'What? No!' As her brain finally stopped freewheeling and the cogs engaged, she put her hand protectively on top of the ices piled up beside her. 'I have to have these today. Now. And the other ices I ordered.' Then felt horribly guilty for putting her own needs first when Ria was in such trouble.

Sorrel had always struggled with Ria's somewhat cavalier attitude to business. She'd done everything she could to organise her but it was like pushing water uphill. If she was in trouble with the taxman, though, she must be frightened to death.

'That would be the champagne sorbet that you can't find,' Alexander said, jerking her back to her own problem.

'Amongst other things.' At least he'd had his ears as well as his eyes open while he'd been ogling her underwear. 'Perhaps they're still in the kitchen freezer?' she suggested, fingers mentally crossed. 'I don't imagine that she would have been thinking too clearly.' Then, furious, 'Why on earth didn't she call me if she was in trouble? She knew I would have helped.'

'She called me.'

'And you came racing, *ventre à terre*, to rescue her?' Her sarcasm covered a momentary pang of envy for such devotion. If he'd been *devoted*, she reminded herself, he'd have been here, supporting her instead of gallivanting around the world, beachcombing, no doubt with obligatory dusky maiden in attendance. Sending Ria the odd postcard when he could be bothered.

'Hardly "belly to the earth". I was in a Boeing at thirty thousand feet,' he replied, picking up on the sarcasm and returning it with interest.

'The modern equivalent,' she snapped back. But he had come. 'So? What are you going to do? Sort things out? Put the business back on a proper footing?' she asked, torn between hope and doubt. What Ria needed was an accountant who couldn't be twisted around her little finger. Not some lotus-eater.

'No. I'm here to shut up shop. Knickerbocker Gloria is no longer trading.'

'But…'

'But what?'

'Never mind.'

She would do her level best to help Ria save her business just as soon as the Jefferson job was over. Right now it was her reputation that was on the line. Without that sorbet, she was toast and she wasn't about to allow Ria's beefcake toy boy to stand in her way.

CHAPTER TWO

Ideas should be clear and ice cream thick. A Spanish Proverb

—from Rosie's 'Little Book of Ice Cream'

'DO YOU MIND?' Sorrel asked, when he didn't move or step aside to allow her through to the preparation room.

Alexander West was considerably taller than her, but not so tall—thanks to her four-inch heels—that she was forced to crick her neck to look him in the eye. A woman in business had to learn to stand her ground and, if she were ever to be made Chancellor of the Exchequer, her first act on taking office would be to make four-inch designer heels a tax-deductible expense.

'Actually, I do,' he said.

Terrific. A businessman would understand, be reasonable. Alexander West might be a travelling man who could, no doubt, make himself understood in a dozen languages, but he wasn't talking hers.

Never mind. She hadn't got this far without becoming multi-lingual herself...

'Please, Mr West...' she began, doing her best to ignore his disintegrating T-shirt, his close-fitting jeans, the scent of warm male skin prickling her nose, loosening her bones...

It was tough being a woman in business. Tough running

events. A woman had to use whatever tools came to hand.
With banks it was her ability to put together a solid business
plan; with clients it was her intuitive understanding of what
they wanted; with uncooperative staff at hotels she occasionally had to resort to the sharp edge of her tongue, but only as
a last resort. The most effective tool in the box she'd always
found to be a smile and this wasn't the moment to hold back.
She gave him the full, wide-screen, Technicolor version she'd
inherited from her mother. The one known in the family as
'the heartbreaker', although in her case the only heart that had
suffered any damage was her own.

'Alexander…' She switched to his first name, needing to
make an ally of him, involve him in her problem. 'This is important.'

She had his attention now and his smile faded until all she
could see was a white starburst of lines around those hot blue
eyes where they had been screwed up against the sun. Like a
tractor-beam in an old science fiction movie, they drew her
towards the seductive curve of his lower lip, pulling her in…

'How important?' he asked. His voice, dangerously soft,
grazed her skin and mesmerized; her breath snagged in her
throat as the warmth of his body wrapped around her. When
had she moved? How had she got close enough to feel his
breath against her cheek?

Bells were clanging a warning somewhere, but her mouth
was so hot that she instinctively touched her lower lip with
her tongue to cool it.

'Really, really…' her voice caught in her throat '…impor-
tant.'

Even as her brain was scrambling an urgent message to her
feet to step back his hand was at her waist, sliding beneath the
skimpy top, spreading across her back, each fingertip sending shivery little sparks of pleasure dancing across her skin.
Arousing drugging sensations that blocked the danger sig-

nals and, as he lowered his mouth to hers, only one word was
making it through.

'Yes...'

It murmured through her body as his lips touched hers, slipping through her defences as smoothly as a silver key turning
in a well-oiled lock. Whispering seduction as his tongue slid
across her lower lip, dipped between her teeth and her body
arched towards him wanting more, wanting him.

She lifted her arms but as she slid them around his neck he
broke the connection, lifting his head a fraction to look at her
for a moment and murmur, 'Not raspberry...'

Not raspberry?

He was frowning a little as he straightened so that he was
looking down at her. Five-inch heels. She needed five-inch
heels...

'And not that important.'

As his hand slid away from her she took a step back,
grabbed behind for the freezer for the second time, steady-
ing herself while her legs remembered what they were for.
And for the second time that morning wished she'd kept her
mouth shut.

'Not important?' No, not *that* important...

Oh, God! Forget raspberry—if she ever blushed she
wouldn't be raspberry, she'd be beetroot. It was the skirt all
over again, only that had been him looking. This had been
her losing all sense as her wayward genes, the curse of all
Amery women, had temporarily asserted themselves and reason, judgement, had flown out of the window. It was that easy
to lose your head.

Just one look and she had wanted him to kiss her. Wanted
a lot more. Stupid, crazy and rare in ways he couldn't begin
to understand, Alexander West had read something entirely
different into her motives. Had thought that she was prepared
to seduce him to get what she wanted...

'It's just ice cream,' he said, dismissively.

Just?

'Did you say "*just* ice cream"?'

Focus on that. Ice…

'How did you get in here?' he demanded, irritably, ignoring the question. 'The shop isn't open.'

The change of mood was like a slap, but it had the effect of jarring her senses back into place.

'I used the side door,' she snapped, almost as shocked by his dismissal of ice cream as something anyone could take seriously as a sizzling kiss that had momentarily stolen her wits. And which he had swept aside as casually.

No way was she going to tell him that Ria had given her a key so that she could collect her orders out of hours. She wasn't going to tell him anything.

It was only the absolute necessity of verifying that Ria had completed her order that kept her from doing the sensible thing and walking out. Once she knew it was there, she could come and pick it up later when he had gone.

'It was locked,' he countered.

'Not when I walked through it.' The truth, the whole truth and very nearly nothing but the truth. 'Unlike the front door. You're not going to get Ria out of trouble if you shut her customers out,' she added, pointedly.

Alexander West gave her a long, thoughtful look—the kind that suggested he knew when he was being flimflammed. He might look as if he were about to fall asleep where he stood, but, as he'd just demonstrated, he was very much awake and apparently leaping to all manner of conclusions.

Not without reason where the key was concerned.

As for the rest…

Wrong, wrong, wrong!

'I did pay for my order in advance,' she said, doing her best to blank out the humming of her pulse, determined to divert his attention from a smile that had got her into so much trouble—and which she'd stow away with the suit, labelled not suitable for office wear, the minute she got home—along with her apparent ability to walk through locked doors. Just in case he took it into his head to use those long fingers, strong capable hands, to do a pat-down search.

Her body practically melted at the thought.

'Maybe,' she said, her voice apparently disconnected from her body and brisk as a brand-new yard broom, 'since you appear to have taken charge in Ria's absence, you could find the rest of it for me?'

Better. Ignore the body. Stick with the voice…

'You paid in advance?'

Much better. He wasn't just diverted, he was seriously surprised and his eyebrows rose, drawing attention to the hair flopping over his forehead and practically falling in his eyes.

Sorrel found herself struggling against the urge to lean into him, to reach up and comb it back with her fingers, feel the strength of that hot body against hers as she put her arms around his neck and fastened it tidily out of the way with an elastic band.

Fortunately, she didn't have a band handy but, not taking any chances, she kept her fingers busy tucking a stray wisp of her own hair behind an ear. Then, just to be safe, she rubbed her thumb over the little ice-cream-cornet earring that had been a birthday gift from her ideal man, Graeme Laing. The well-groomed, totally focused man for whom travelling meant brief business trips to Zurich, New York or Hong Kong.

Travelling for business was okay.

'It is normal business practice,' she assured him.

'"Normal" and "business practice" are not words I've ever heard Ria use in the same sentence,' Alexander replied.

'That I can believe, but I'm not Ria.'

'No?' Her assertion didn't impress him. He didn't even

ask what kind of business she was in. Clearly his interest in her didn't stretch further than her underwear. He had to have known—his kiss had left her clinging to the freezer for support, for heaven's sake—that she had been lost to reality, but he hadn't bothered to follow through, press his advantage.

He'd simply been proving the point that she would do anything to get her ice cream.

He had been wrong about that, too. She hadn't been thinking about her order, or the major event that depended upon it. She hadn't been thinking at all, only feeling the fizz of heat rushing through her veins, a shocking need to be kissed, to be touched…

She cut off the thought, aware that she should be grateful that he hadn't taken advantage of her incomprehensible meltdown.

She *was* grateful.

Having got over his shock at Ria's unaccountable lapse into efficiency, however, Alexander shrugged and the gap along his shoulder seam widened, putting her fledgling gratitude to the test.

'Okay,' he said. 'Show me a receipt and you can take your ices.'

'A receipt?'

That took her mind off his disintegrating clothing, and the sudden chill around her midriff had nothing to do with the fact that she was leaning against an open freezer.

'It is normal business practice to issue one,' he said.

She couldn't be certain that he was mocking her, but it felt very much like it. He was pretty sharp for a man with such a louche lifestyle, but presumably financing it required a certain amount of ruthlessness. Was that why he felt responsible for Ria's problems? She was full of life, looked fabulous for forty, but good-looking toy-boy lovers—no matter how occasional—were an expensive luxury.

'You do have one?'

'A receipt? Not with me,' she hedged, unwilling to admit to her own rare lapse in efficiency. 'Ria will have entered the payment in her books,' she pointed out.

'Ria hasn't made an entry in her books for weeks.'

'But that's—'

'That's Ria.'

'It's as bad as that?' she asked.

'Worse.'

Sorrel groaned. 'She's hopeless with the practicalities. I have to write down the ingredients when we experiment with flavours for ice cream, but even then you never know what extra little touch she's going to toss in as an afterthought the minute your back is turned.'

'It's the extra little touch that makes the magic.'

'True,' she said, surprised that someone who thought ice cream unimportant would know that. 'Sadly, there's no guarantee that it will be the same touch.' While she wanted the magic, she also needed consistency. Ria preferred the serendipitous joy of stumbling on some exciting new flavour, which made a visit to Knickerbocker Gloria—the glorious step-back-in-time ice-cream parlour that was at the heart of the business—something of an adventure. Or deeply frustrating if you came back hoping for a second helping of an ice cream you'd fallen in love with. Fortunately for the business, the adventure mostly outweighed the frustration.

Mostly.

'You have to learn to live with the risk or move on,' Alexander said, apparently able to read her mind.

'Do I?' She regarded him with the same thoughtful look that he had turned on her. 'Is it the risk that brings you back?' she asked.

His smile was a dangerous thing. Fleeting. Filled with ambiguity. Was he amused? She couldn't be certain. And if he was, was he laughing at himself or at her pathetic attempt to tease information out of him? Why did it matter? His relationship with Ria had nothing to do with her unless it interfered with her business.

It was interfering with her business right now.

He was standing in the way of what she needed, but she needed his co-operation. In a moment of weakness, she had allowed her concentration to slip, but she wouldn't let that happen again. She didn't care what had brought Alexander West flying back to Maybridge, to Ria. She only cared about the needs of her own business.

'When it comes to ice cream,' she said, not waiting for an answer, 'Ria's individuality is my biggest selling point.'

Having practically torn her hair out at Ria's inability to stick to a recipe, she had finally taken the line of least resistance, offering something unrepeatable—colours and flavours that were individually tailored to her clients' personal requirements—to sell the uniqueness of her ices.

It did mean that she had to work closely with Ria, recording her recipes at the moment of creation to ensure that she delivered the ices that her client tasted and approved and didn't go off on some last-minute fantasy version conjured up in a flash of inspiration. It wasn't easy, she couldn't be here all the time, but it had been worth the effort.

'Where is Ria?' she asked, again. 'And where's Nancy?' She glanced at her watch. 'She has to drop her daughter off at school, but she should have been here an hour ago to open up the ice-cream parlour.'

'She was, but, since there's no possibility that the business will continue, it seemed kinder to suggest she use her time to explore other employment opportunities.'

'Kinder?' He'd fired her? Things were moving a lot faster than she had anticipated. *'Kinder?'* she repeated. 'Have you any idea how important this job is to Nancy? She's a single mother. Finding another job—'

'Take it up with Ria,' he said, cutting her off in full flow. 'She's the one who's disappeared.'

'Disappeared?' For a man so relaxed that he looked as if he might slide down the door at any minute, he moved with lightning speed. That capable hand was at her elbow as the blood drained from her face and long before the wobble reached her knees. 'What do you mean, disappeared?'

'Nothing. Bad choice of words.' He knew, she thought. He understood that beneath Ria's vivid clothes, her life-embracing exuberance, there was a fragility…

He was close again and she caught the scent of the lavender that Ria cut from her garden and laid between her sheets. Ria… This was about her, she reminded herself. 'She can't hide from the taxman.'

'No, but, if you know her as well as you say, you'll know that when things get tough, she does a good impression of an ostrich.'

That rang true. Ria was very good at sticking her head in the sand and not hearing anything she didn't want to know. Such as advice about being more organised. About consistency in the flavours she sold in the ice-cream parlour, saving the experimental flavours for 'specials'. 'Have you any idea which beach she might have chosen? To bury her head in.'

'That's not your concern.'

No. At least it was, but she knew what he meant. Since Ria had left him in charge he must have spoken to her and doubtless knew a lot more than he was saying.

'I've been trying to organise her,' she said, bitterly regretting that she hadn't tried harder. She might not approve of the 'postcard' man, but she hated him thinking that she didn't care. 'It's like trying to herd cats.'

That won her a smile that she could read. Wry, a touch conspiratorial, a moment shared between two people who knew all Ria's faults and, despite her determination not to, she found herself smiling back.

'Tell me about it,' he murmured, then, as she shivered again, 'Are you okay?'

'Absolutely.' But as her eyes met his the wobble intensified and she hadn't a clue what she was feeling; only that 'okay' wasn't it. Alexander West was too physical, too male, too close. He was taking liberties with her sense of purpose, with her ability to think and act clearly in a crisis. 'I'm just a bit off balance,' she said. 'I've had my head in the freezer for too long. I stood up too fast...'

'That will do it every time.'

His expression was serious, but his eyes were telling a different story.

'Yes...' That and a warm hand cradling her elbow, eyes the colour of the sea on a blue-sky day. A shared concern about a friend. 'Tell me what you know,' she said, this time to distract herself.

He shook his head. 'Not much. I got back late last night. The key was under the doormat.'

'The key? I assumed...' She assumed that Ria would have been on the doorstep with open arms. 'Are you telling me that you haven't seen her?' He shook his head and the sunlight streaming in from the small window above the door glinted on the golden streaks in his hair. 'But you have spoken to her? What exactly did she say?'

'There was an electric storm and the line kept breaking up. It's taken me three days to get home and she was long gone by the time I got here.'

Three days? He'd been travelling for three days? Where in the world had he been? And how much must he care if he'd travel that distance to come to her rescue? She crushed the thought. She wasn't interested in him or where he'd come from.

'Where? Where has she gone?'

'I've no idea.'

'Someone must know where she is,' she objected. 'She wouldn't have left her cats to fend for themselves.'

That provoked another of those fleeting smiles. 'Arthur and Guinevere are comfortably tucked up with a neighbour who is under the impression that Ria is dealing with a family emergency.'

'I didn't think she had any family.'

'No?' He said that as if he knew something that she didn't. He didn't elaborate, but said, 'This isn't the first time she's done this.'

'Oh?' That wasn't good news.

'She's had a couple of close calls in the past. I had hoped, after the last time, she'd learned her lesson. I did warn her…' Warn her? 'It's not fair on the people who rely on her. Suppliers, customers…' Perhaps realising that he was leaving himself open to an appeal from her, he stopped. 'She knows what's going to happen and doesn't want to be around to witness it.'

'Are you sure?'

'Why else would she have taken off?'

Sorrel shook her head. He was right. There was no other explanation.

'In the meantime nothing can leave here until I've made an inventory of the assets.' As if to make his point, he finally moved and began returning the large containers of ice cream to the freezer.

'Hold on! These aren't *assets*.' Sorrel grabbed the one containing tiny chocolate-cupcake cases filled with raspberry gelato. 'These are mine. I told you, I've already paid for them.'

'How? Cheque, credit card? I've been to the bank and Ria hasn't paid anything in for weeks.'

She blinked. The bank had talked to him about Ria's account? They wouldn't do that unless it was a joint account. Or he had a power of attorney to act on her behalf. Was that what Ria had left for him?

She didn't ask. He wouldn't tell her and besides she had more than enough problems of her own right now. And the biggest of them was waiting for an answer to his question.

'Not a cheque,' she said. 'Who carries a cheque book these days?' He waited. 'I, um, gave her...' She hesitated, well aware how stupid she was going to look.

'Please tell me you didn't give her cash,' he said, way ahead of her.

It had been a rare, uncharacteristic lapse from the strictest standards she applied to her business, but the circumstances had been rare, too. Alexander had no way of knowing that and with a little shrug, a wry smile that she hoped would tempt a little understanding, she said, 'I will if you insist, but it won't alter the fact.'

'Then I hope,' he said, not responding to the smile, 'that you kept the receipt in a safe place.'

She had hoped he'd forgotten about the receipt. Clearly not.

Brisk, businesslike...

Busted.

CHAPTER THREE

*There are four basic food groups; you'll find them all
in a Knickerbocker Glory.*
—*from Rosie's 'Little Book of Ice Cream'*

'I WAS IN A RUSH. There was an emergency.' It was no excuse,
Sorrel knew, but you had to have been there. 'I told her she
could give me the receipt when I picked up the order.'

He didn't say anything—he clearly wasn't a man to strain
himself—but an infinitesimal lift of his eyebrows left her in
no doubt what he was thinking.

'Don't look at me like that!'

No, no, no… Get a grip. You're the professional, he's the…

She wasn't sure what he was. Only that he was trouble in
capitals from T through to E.

'I'd called in to tell Ria that the Jefferson contract was
signed,' she said, determined to explain, show him that she
wasn't the complete idiot that, with absolutely no justification, he clearly thought her. That was twice he'd got her totally wrong and he didn't even know her name… 'I had the
list of ices the client had chosen and we were going through
it when my brother-in-law called to tell me that my sister had
been rushed into Maybridge General.' His face remained ex-
pressionless. 'As I was leaving, Ria asked if she could have
some cash upfront. It was a big order,' she added.

'How big?' She told him and the eyebrows reacted with rather more energy. 'How much ice cream did you order, for heaven's sake?'

So. That was what it took to rouse him. Money.

Why was she surprised?

'A lot, but it's not just the quantity,' she told him, 'it's the quality. These ices aren't like the stuff she sells in Knickerbocker Gloria, lovely though that is.' Having finally got his attention, she wasn't about to lose the opportunity to state her case. 'Certainly nothing like the stuff that gets swirled into a cornet from our van.'

'You have an ice-cream round?'

Oh, Lord, now he thought she was flogging the stuff from a van on the streets.

'No. We have a vintage ice cream van. Rosie. She's a bit of a celebrity since she started making a regular appearance in a television soap opera.' Put that on a postcard home, Alexander West.

'Rosie?'

'She's pink.' He didn't exactly roll his eyes, but he might as well have done. So much for making an impression. 'The ices we commission from Ria are for adults,' she continued, determined to convince him that she wasn't some flaky lightweight running a cash-in-hand, fly-by-night company. 'They need expensive ingredients. Organic fruit. Liqueurs.'

'And champagne.'

'And champagne,' she agreed. 'Not some fizzy substitute, but the real thing. It's a big outlay, especially when things are tight.'

'So? What was the problem with your debit card?'

'Nothing. Ria's card machine was playing up and, since I couldn't wait, I dashed across the road to the ATM.'

'You fell for that?' he asked in a way that suggested she

could wave goodbye to her credibility as it flew out of the window.

Sorrel let slip an expletive. He was right. She was an idiot.

Not even her soft-as-butter sister, Elle, would have been taken in by that old chestnut. But this was Ria! Okay, she was as organised as a boxful of kittens, but so warm, so full of love.

So like her own mother.

Right down to her unfortunate taste in men.

She sighed. Enough said. Lesson learned. Move on. But it was time to put this exchange on a business footing. Alexander West hadn't bothered to ask who she was, no doubt hoping he could shoo her out of the door quick sharp, and forget that she existed.

Time to let him know that it wasn't going to happen.

'How is your sister?' he asked, before she could tell him so. 'You said she was rushed into hospital? Was it serious?'

'Serious?' She blinked. Hadn't she said?

Apparently not. Well, his concern demonstrated thoughtfulness. Or did he think it was just an excuse to cover her stupidity? The latter, she was almost sure...

'Incurable,' she replied, just to see shock replacing the smug male expression that practically shouted, *'Got you...'* 'It's called motherhood. She had a girl—Fenny Louise, seven pounds, six ounces—practically on the hospital steps. Her third.' She offered him her hand. 'I know who you are, Mr West, but you don't know me.' Despite a kiss that was still sizzling quietly under her skin, ready to re-ignite at the slightest encouragement. 'Sorrel Amery. I'm the CEO of Scoop!'

Her hand, which had been resting protectively on the frosted container, was ice cold, a fact she realised the minute he took it and heat rocketed up to her shoulder before spiralling down into parts that a simple handshake shouldn't reach.

Was he plugged into the National Grid?

'Scoop?' There went the eyebrow again.

'It's not a question,' she informed him, briskly, retrieving the hand rather more quickly than was polite. 'It's an exclamation.' She began to return the containers to the freezer before both she and their contents melted. None of them were going anywhere in the immediate future. 'We deliver an ice-cream experience for special events. Weddings, receptions, parties,' she explained. 'This order is for a tennis party Jefferson Sports are hosting at Cranbrook Park to show their new range of summer sports clothing and equipment in action to the lifestyle press. The house has recently been restored,' she added, 'and converted into a hotel and conference centre.'

'Jefferson Sports?'

'They're a major local company. Manufacturers and retailers of high-end sports gear, and clothing. Camping equipment…'

'I know who they are.'

'Then you'll understand the importance of this order,' she said, determined to press the advantage now that she had snagged his interest. 'It's a media event. The idea is that the gossip magazines and women's pages will publish a lot of pretty pictures, which will get everyone rushing out to buy the sexy new racquets, pink tennis balls and the clothes that the tennis stars will be wearing at Wimbledon this year.'

'Pink?'

'Pink, mauve, blue…designer colours to match your outfit.'

'Please tell me that you're kidding.'

'You think there will be outrage?' She risked a smile—just a low-wattage affair. 'Letters to *The Times*? Questions raised about the legality of the balls? All bags of publicity for Jefferson Sports.'

'Always assuming that it doesn't rain.'

'The forecast is good, but there's a picturesque Victorian Conservatory, a classical temple, a large marquee and a load of celebrities. The pictures will be great whatever the weather.'

She'd seized the opportunity to promote their company to Nick Jefferson when he'd called at her office to book 'Rosie' for his youngest child's birthday party. Rosie had been a hit and, when he'd invited her to tender for this promotional party, she'd beaten off the competition with her idea for a 'champagne tea' delivered in mouth-sized bites of ice cream—witty, summery, fun.

There were going to be major sports stars amongst the guests, all the usual 'celebrities' as well as a couple of minor royals, and the coverage in the gossip magazines and Sunday newspapers would give them exposure to their core customer base that not even the biggest advertising budget could deliver.

Without Ria's ices she would not only miss that opportunity, but, if she didn't deliver, her reputation would be in ruins and all her hard work would have been for nothing.

'Mr West…' calling him Alexander hadn't worked and she was in dead earnest now; it was vital to convince him '…if I don't deliver a perfectly executed event for Jefferson my reputation will disappear faster than a choc ice in a heatwave.' Worse, it could backfire on the rest of the business. 'If that happens, Ria won't be the only one up the financial creek without a paddle and…' since he'd already admitted that he was in some way responsible for Ria's problems there was no harm in playing the guilt card '…you'll have two insolvencies on your conscience.'

'If you relied on Ria,' he replied, unmoved, 'you deserve to sink.'

'That's a bit harsh.' She had always been aware that there was an element of risk working with Ria, but until now she'd been managing it. Or thought she had.

'It's a harsh world.'

'So you're going to let the taxman take us both down?'

'If we don't pay our taxes, Miss Amery, everyone loses.'

'I pay mine!' she declared, furiously. 'On the dot. Along with all my bills. What about you?'

'What about me?'

'Well, you're never here, are you? Do you have a job, Mr West, or do you just live on handouts from gullible women?'

'Is that what you think? That I'm the reason Ria is in trouble?'

His voice, soft as cobwebs, raised the gooseflesh on her arms. Had she got it totally wrong?

Renowned for being calm in a crisis, she was totally losing it in the face of the kind of body that challenged her notion of what was attractive in a man. Slim, elegant, wearing bespoke tailoring...

He was so not her type!

Not in a million years.

She mentally hung a Do Not Touch notice around his neck, counted to three and took a deep breath.

'It doesn't matter what I think.' The ability to hang on to a calm demeanour in the face of disaster was a prime requisite of the events organiser, but right now she was running on her reserve tank with the red light flashing a warning. 'Can we at least check and see if she's made the sorbet?' she suggested, resisting the urge to rub her hands up and down her arms to warm them and instead reaching for a white coat and slipping it on. Settling a white trilby over her hair. A statement of intent. 'It has a very short shelf life and by the time you and the Revenue sort out the paperwork it will be well beyond its best-before date. So much sorbet down the drain. A waste of everyone's money.'

'I'm sure you're only worried about yours.'

He was losing patience now, regarding her with undisguised irritation, and she regretted her rush to cover up. The slightest shrug would have sent a strap sliding from her shoulder.

It wasn't the way she did business, but then he wasn't the

kind of man she usually did business with. Any distraction in a crisis… Now she was aware of the danger she would stay well out of reach.

'If you insist,' she continued, using the only other way of grabbing his attention that was open to her, 'I'll pay for it again.' Heavy stress on the "again". 'I'd rather lose money on this event than my reputation.'

He didn't leap to accept her offer despite the fact that it would help pay the outstanding tax bill.

'That would be in cash, too, of course.' And, since this was her mistake, it would be taken from her own bank account. She would have to forget all about that pair of pink Miu Miu sandals at the top of her shoe wish-list. There were always more shoes, but there was only one Scoop! Her sister had created it and she wasn't going to be the one to lose it. 'Since Ria's bank account has presumably been frozen,' she added, as a face-saving sop to his pride.

She assumed it would go straight into his back pocket but she'd already insulted him once—in response to gravest provocation—and doing it again wasn't going to get her what she wanted.

She held her breath and, after what felt like a lifetime, he moved to one side to allow her to pass.

She crushed her disappointment that cash would move him when her appeal to his sense of fair play had failed. That a lovely woman should be in thrall to a man so unworthy of her. Not that she was surprised. She'd suffered the consequences of men who took advantage of foolish women.

Wouldn't be here but for one of them.

Once they'd checked the drawers of the upright freezers in the kitchen, however, she had a bigger problem than Ria's inevitably doomed love affair to worry about.

'No sorbet,' Alexander said, without any discernible expression of surprise, 'and no cucumber ice cream, although I can't bring myself to believe that's a bad thing.'

'Savoury ice cream is very fashionable,' she said, more concerned about how long it would take her to make the missing ices than whether he approved of her flavour choices.

'I rest my case,' he replied, clearly believing that they were done. 'You can take the ices you say are yours, Miss Amery. I won't take your money, but I will have your key before you go.'

He held out his hand. She ignored it. She wasn't done here. Not by a long chalk. But since he was in control of the ice-cream parlour, he was the one she had to convince to allow her to stay.

'What will it take?' she asked, looking around at the gleaming kitchen. 'To keep Knickerbocker Gloria going?'

'It's not going to happen.'

She frowned. 'That's hardly your decision, surely?'

'There's no one else here.'

'And closing it is your best shot?'

'It would take a large injection of cash to settle with the creditors and someone with a firm grip on the paperwork at the helm.' He didn't look or sound optimistic. Actually, he looked as if he was about to go to sleep propped up against the freezer door.

'How much cash?'

'Why?' He was regarding her sleepily from beneath heavy-lidded eyes that looked as if they could barely stay open, but she wasn't fooled for a minute. She had his full attention. 'Don't tell me you're interested.'

'Why not?' He didn't answer, but she hadn't expected him to. He had her down as an idiot who thought she could get what she wanted in business by flirting. A rare mistake. Now she was going to have to work twice as hard to convince him otherwise. 'At the right price I could be very interested, although on this occasion,' she added, 'I won't be paying in cash and will definitely require a receipt.'

Sorrel heard the words, knew they had come from her mouth, but still didn't believe it. She didn't make snap decisions. She planned things through, carefully assessed the potential, worked out the cost-benefit ratio. And always talked to her financial advisor before making any decision that would affect her carefully constructed five-year plan.

Not that she had to talk to Graeme to know exactly what he would say.

The words 'do not touch' and 'bargepole' would be closely linked, followed by a silence filled with an unspoken 'I told you so'. He had never approved of Ria.

Maybe, if she laughed, Alexander West would think she'd been joking.

'You're a fast learner,' he said. 'I'll give you that.'

Too late.

'How generous.' Possibly. Of course, it could have been sarcasm since he wasn't excited enough by her interest to do more than lean a little more heavily against the freezer. For a man whose aim in life was to keep moving, he certainly didn't believe in wasting energy. Presumably his exploration was confined to the local bars set beneath palm trees on those lovely beaches.

'What kind of figure were you thinking of offering?' he asked.

Thinking? This was not her day for thinking…

'I'll need to see the accounts before I'm prepared to talk about an offer,' she said, her brain beginning to catch up with her mouth. 'How long is the lease? Do you know?'

'It's not transferable. You'd have to negotiate a new lease with the landlord.'

'Oh…' She was surprised he knew that, but then it had been that kind of day. Full of surprises. None of them, so far, good. 'No doubt he'll take the opportunity to increase the rent. They've been low at this end of the High Street but footfall has picked up in the last couple of years.' There had been a major improvement project with an influx of small specialist shops attracting shoppers who were looking for something different and were prepared to pay for quality. Knickerbocker Gloria had been a vanguard of that movement and had done well out of it. Very well. Which made the sudden collapse all the more surprising. 'No doubt he'll want to take advantage of that.'

'It's taken a lot of money to improve this part of the town. He's entitled to reap the benefit, don't you think?'

'I suppose so. Who is the landlord?' she asked. 'Do you know?'

'Yes.' The corner of his mouth lifted a fraction. 'I am.'

With her entire focus centred on the tiny crease that formed as the embryonic smile took form, grew into a teasing quirk, her certainty on the putty question was undermined by a distinct slackening around her knees and it took a moment for his words to sink in.

He was…

What?

'Oh…Knickerbocker Gloria…' She pulled a face. 'So that's my foot in my mouth right up to the ankle, then?'

The smile deepened. 'I'll bear in mind what you said about increasing the rent.'

'Terrific.' She was having a bad day and then some.

'I'm always open to negotiation. For the right tenant.'

'Is that how Ria managed to get such a good deal?' she asked.

'Good deal?'

He didn't move, but her skin began to tingle and her mouth dried…

'Her rent is very…reasonable.' There was no point dodging the bullet. The words had come out of her mouth even if she hadn't meant them in quite the way they'd sounded. Or maybe she had. The thought of Ria haggling over money was too ridiculous to contemplate. 'Even for the wrong end of the High Street.'

'Let me get this right,' he said. 'You're moving from the suggestion that she's paying me for services rendered, to me subsidising her, likewise?'

There were days when you just shouldn't get out of bed. This was rapidly turning into one of them.

Forget ankle. They were talking knee and beyond.

'You're not…?' she said, unable to actually put the thought into words.

'I'm not. She's not. I don't understand why you'd think we were.' His eyebrow rose questioningly.

'The fact that she sent for you when she was in trouble and you came,' she suggested.

'We've known one another a long time.'

She shook her head. 'It's more than that.'

His shoulders shifted in an awkward shrug that in anyone else she would have put down to embarrassment. 'I have a responsibility to her.'

'Because you're her landlord?'

'It's more complicated than that.'

'I don't doubt it. I found her weeping over the last card you sent her.'

'Damn.' He sighed. 'That wasn't about me but it does begin to explain what's been happening here.'

'Does it?' She waited but he was lost in thought. 'When can I see the accounts?' she asked, finally.

He came back from wherever he'd been in his head. 'You're serious?'

'Don't I look serious?'

'Seriously?' He took a long, slow look that began at her shoes, travelled up the length of the white coat with a long pause at her cleavage before coming to a rest on the unflattering hat. 'Sorry,' he said finally, reaching out and removing the offending headgear. 'There is no way I can take you seriously in this thing.'

'Seriously,' she repeated, not so much as blinking despite a heartbeat that was racketing out of control at the intimacy of such a gesture. The man was an oaf—albeit a sexy oaf—and she refused to let him fluster her. Okay, it was too late for that; she was flustered beyond recovery, but she couldn't—wouldn't—allow him to see that.

He shrugged. 'Seriously? You look like someone who said the first thing that came into her head.'

'That is something I never do.' Or hadn't… Until now.

Like the kiss, it was an aberration.

A one-off.

Not to be repeated.

It was turning into quite a morning for firsts. None of them good.

'On the form you've shown so far, I'd suggest that you never think before you speak.'

He might have a point about that. At least where he was concerned. She'd been leaping to conclusions and speaking before her brain was engaged ever since she'd turned from the freezer and seen him watching her.

His attention was all on her now as he spun the hat teasingly on a finger. She snatched it back but didn't put it back on her head.

'I'm having an off day,' she said.

'Just the one? You'll forgive me if I suggest that on present form you're not capable of running the business you already have, let alone taking on one encumbered by debt.'

'Actually, I won't, if it's all the same to you.' Her offer might have been somewhat rash, but she wasn't going to let him slouch there and judge her on a completely uncharacteristic performance. He might have got closer to her than any man since Jamie Coolidge had done her the favour of relieving her of her virginity when she was seventeen, but he knew nothing about her. 'My competence is no concern of yours. If I go to the wall, I won't be texting you to come and rescue me.'

'I have your word on that?'

'Cross my heart and spit in your eye,' she said, ignoring the shivery sensation that seemed to have taken up residence in her spine.

'Crossing your fingers might be more useful,' he suggested.

'I can't create a spreadsheet with my fingers crossed,' she pointed out, sticking to the practicalities. The practicalities never answered back, never let you down, never took the fast road out of town... 'You have to admit, this is the obvious answer to both our problems.'

'I'm admitting nothing. Surely you could get your ice cream made somewhere else?' he persisted. 'You said that you have the recipes.'

'Some of them,' she admitted. Not nearly enough. Not the chocolate chilli ice Ria was supposed to deliver for a corporate shindig the following week. And they were experimenting with an orange sorbet for a wedding. She needed samples so that the bride could choose. 'But I need more than recipes. I need equipment.'

'Not much. Ria began making ices in the kitchen at home.'

'Did she?' How long ago was that? How long had Ria and Alexander known one another? It was always harder to pin an age on a man. They hit a peak at around thirty and, if they looked after themselves, didn't start to sag until well into middle age, which was grossly unfair. He was definitely at a peak... Down, girl! 'Are you suggesting that I might do the same?'

'Why not?'

'Perhaps because I'm not running a cottage industry, but a

high-end events company?' she replied. 'And, since my ices are for public consumption, they have to be prepared in a kitchen that has been inspected and licensed by the Environmental Health Officer rather than one that closely resembles an annexe to the local animal shelter.'

'Animal shelter?' His bark of laughter took her by surprise. 'For a moment you had me believing you.'

'The animals are my sister's province.'

'Babies and animals? She has her hands full.'

'A different sister.'

'There are *three* of you?' he asked, apparently astonished.

'Congratulations, Mr West. You can do simple arithmetic.'

'When pushed,' he admitted. 'My concern is whether the world can take you times three.'

So rude!

'No need to worry on the world's account,' she replied. 'My mother dipped into a wide gene pool and we are not in the least bit alike in looks or temperament.'

She could see him thinking about that and then making the decision not to go there.

'Wouldn't sister number three give you a hand scrubbing the kitchen down?' he asked. He was beginning to sound a touch desperate. 'Who would know?'

'I would,' she said, her determination growing in direct proportion to his resistance. As a last resort she could probably use the kitchens at Haughton Manor, but they didn't have an ice-cream maker and why should she be put to even more inconvenience when she had a custom-built facility right here? 'Anyone would think you don't want me to rescue Knickerbocker Gloria.'

'Anyone would be right,' he replied. 'I don't.'

CHAPTER FOUR

Man cannot live on ice cream alone. Women are tougher.
—from Rosie's 'Little Book of Ice Cream'

SORREL WAS MOMENTARILY taken aback by his frankness. But only momentarily.

'Fortunately, Mr West, that's not your decision to make. I'm sure Her Majesty's Revenue and Customs would be more than happy to negotiate with me if it means they'll get their back taxes paid.' She paused, briefly, but not long enough for him to respond. 'You are aware that fines for non-payment are levied on a daily basis?'

'I had heard a rumour to that effect.'

'And, for your information, while I do keep records of the recipes that Ria has developed for my clients, they are her intellectual copyright. I can't just hand them over to another ice-cream manufacturer and ask them to knock me up a batch.'

Always assuming she could find one who could be bothered.

It hadn't been easy to find anyone prepared to work with her to create her very special requirements. Sorbets tinted to exactly match the embroidery on a bride's gown. Ices the colours of a company logo, or a football-team strip. Who wouldn't suggest she needed her head examined when asked to produce the ice cream equivalent of a cucumber sandwich, but accepted the challenge with childlike glee.

And even if she had been that unscrupulous, there was no way she'd allow herself to be put in this position again. If Knickerbocker Gloria folded she would have to set up her own production plant from scratch. It would take time to find the right premises, source equipment, train staff and be inspected before she could be up and running. And time was the one thing she didn't have.

And she'd still be missing the one vital ingredient that made what she offered so special. Ria.

She might very well have said the first thing that came into her head, but taking over Knickerbocker Gloria, putting it on a proper, well-managed footing, could save both Ria and Scoop! And if, in the process, she wiped that patronising expression from Alexander West's face, then it would be worth it.

'Not without her permission,' she added. 'And unless you can tell me where she is right now that is a non-starter.'

'Why?'

'Because the Jefferson party is tomorrow.'

'Tomorrow!' Now she had his attention.

'I believe I mentioned that the sorbet has a very short shelf life.'

'So you did.'

'I wasn't sure that you were listening.'

'I promise you,' he said, 'you've had my undivided attention from the moment you walked in.'

'Yes, I had noticed.'

'If you will go around half dressed…'

Half dressed?

'This is not half dressed! On the contrary. I'm wearing a vintage Mary Quant suit that belonged to my grandmother!'

'Not all of it, surely?'

'The jacket is in my van. I didn't expect to be more than

five minutes. Now, are there any more comments you'd like to make about my clothes, the hygiene headgear designed by someone who hates women or the way I run my business? Or can we get on?'

He raised his hands defensively. Then, clearly with some kind of death wish, said, 'Your grandmother?'

'She was a deb in the sixties. Vidal Sassoon hair, Mini car, miniskirts and, supposedly, the liberation of women.'

'Supposedly?'

'Since I've met you, I've discovered that we still have a long way to go. And, while we're putting things straight, this is probably a good time to mention that any negotiations to purchase the business will be conditional on the completion of the Jefferson order.'

'In other words,' he said, grabbing the opportunity to get back to business, 'you're just stalling me out.' He leaned back against the freezer, crossing his sinewy arms so that the muscles bunched in his biceps, tightening the sleeves of his T-shirt again. They looked so...*hard*. It was difficult to resist the urge to touch... 'Until you've got what you want,' he added.

'No!' She curled her fingers tightly into her palms. Well maybe. 'Until I can talk to Ria.'

She knew Ria had friends in Wales from her old travelling days. She went back a couple of times a year and was probably holed up with them in a yurt, drinking nettle beer, eating goat cheese and picking wild herbs for a salad. A place that Sorrel knew, having tried to contact her there back in the summer, didn't have a mobile-phone signal.

Right now, though, she had to deal with her gatekeeper, Alexander West. It was time to stop drooling like a teenager and act like a smart businesswoman.

'I'll rent the premises by the week while we negotiate terms. I will expect anything that I pay to be deducted from the sale price, of course.' He didn't move. 'I'm sure the Revenue would be happy to recover at least a portion of the money owed? Or were you planning on paying it yourself?'

His silence was all the answer she needed.

'So? Do we have a deal?' she asked. 'Because right now I'm firefighting a crisis that isn't of my making and I'd really like to get on with it.'

Even as she said it she knew that wasn't the whole truth. She was supposed to be the whiz-kid entrepreneur. It was her responsibility to ensure that delivery of the product was never compromised and it had been her intention to find a back-up supplier for Scoop!—one that could match Ria's quality, her imagination, her passion.

Unfortunately, there wasn't anyone. At least not locally.

She'd done the rounds when she'd decided to launch this side of the business, looking for someone who would work with her to create the flavours, colours and quality that she wanted to offer her clients. But these were small, one-off, time-consuming special orders and only Ria had been interested.

'Is there really no way of keeping Knickerbocker Gloria as a going concern?' she asked, when he remained silent. 'I really need Ria.'

'Make me an offer I can't refuse,' he said, 'and you can offer her a job.'

He shrugged as if that were it. Game over. He was wrong.

What she had in mind was a partnership. If she took care of the paperwork, kept the books in order, handled the finances— her strengths—Ria would be free to do what she did best.

'Maybe I can come up with an offer *she* can't refuse,' she replied.

'Don't count on it.' He finally pushed himself away from the freezer door, very tall and much too close. While she was sending a frantic message to her feet to move, step back out of the danger zone, he reached forward, took the hat from her hands and set it on her head at a jaunty angle, captured a stray curl that had a mind of its own and tucked it behind her ear, holding it there for a moment as if he knew that it would spring back the moment he let go. Then he shook his head. 'You'd be better off with your hair in a net.'

'Yes…' Her mouth, dry as an August ditch, made all the right moves but no sound came out. She tried harder. 'You're right. I'll see if I can find one. Thank—'

'Don't thank me. Nothing has changed. It's just your good luck that I know Nick Jefferson.' And it was Alexander who took a step back. 'I'm doing this for him, not you, so you'd better deliver the best damn champagne sorbet ever.'

'Or what?' she asked. Clearly saying the first thing that came into her head was habit forming.

'Or you'll answer to me.'

Promises, promises…

The thought whispered through her mind but in the time it took for the connections to snap into action, for her brain to wonder what he'd do if she failed to deliver, Alexander West was back in the office with the door closed, leaving her alone in the prep room.

Probably a good thing, she decided, sliding her fingers behind her ear, where the warmth of his hand still lingered.

Definitely a good thing.

She might have inherited come-day-go-day genes from both her parents, but she had her life mapped out and there was no way she was following her mother down that particular path. Certainly not with a man who, like her father, would be gone long before they'd reached the first stile. Back to his beach-bum lifestyle. Funded by the rent Ria paid for this shop, no doubt. Except she probably owed him money, too. Was that what had brought him flying back? The chance to get her out and install a new tenant at a higher rent?

* * *

While Sorrel Amery had been beguiling him with a smile that had gone straight to his knees, Alexander's coffee had gone cold. He drank it anyway. The alternative was going back out into the preparation room to refill the coffee machine, something he was not prepared to do with Ms Amery in residence.

A hot body, a sexy mouth, and with enough wit to fill his nights back in civilisation very satisfactorily—he would normally have been happy to follow through on a no-holds-barred kiss that had come out of nowhere. She was perfect. In every imaginable way. Even down to the glowing chestnut hair for which she'd presumably been named.

Jet-lagged, tired, as he was, she'd turned him on as if she'd flipped a light switch, but while his body might be urging him to go for it, take what was so clearly on offer, he had a week at most to put this right, catch up with his own paperwork and get back to work. And despite what she clearly thought, he didn't mix business with pleasure—he would be leaving again in days and he'd given up on one-night stands. Anything more needed constant care and feeding and he didn't stay in one place long enough to put in the work.

He pushed the thought away and concentrated on the immediate problem. Not difficult. The problem would be not thinking about her...

What on earth someone as grounded as Nick Jefferson was doing letting Sorrel Amery loose on an important product promotion, he could not imagine.

Cucumber ice cream, for heaven's sake! He shook his head. It had to be the work of some idiot in Jefferson's marketing department; an idiot with a weakness for chestnut hair, translucent skin and legs up to her armpits. No doubt she'd turned on that straight-to-hell smile and the poor sucker had gone down without a fight. Or maybe she had. She'd gone from nought to fifty in second gear and he'd barely touched her...

The thought shivered through him.

He hated it.

Wanted it.

Wanted her with that hot mouth on him, those long legs wrapped around him…

He dragged his hands over his face, rubbed hard in an effort to stimulate the circulation and tear his thoughts away from the bright chestnut curl he'd tucked behind a very pretty ear decorated with a small cream and gold enamelled ice cream cone. There was no denying that everything about her was positively edible, but he wasn't having her for dessert.

She could have a week to make her sorbet and sort out some other arrangement to make her ice cream. He would be concentrating on winding up the business.

He didn't have much time.

Ria's lows were countered by soaring highs and it wouldn't be long before she was having second thoughts. In the meantime, he had no choice but to treat Sorrel Amery like the rest of the creditors and dig her out of the hole she'd been dumped in.

A tap on the door reminded him that in her case it would take more than a cheque to make her disappear. As if to rub in the message, she didn't wait for an invitation. 'I'm sorry to disturb you, but I need Nancy's phone number.'

'Help yourself,' he said, keeping his head down, determined to keep his distance. He picked up an envelope and slit it open, focusing on the job in hand.

'Have you seen…?'

He pointed the letter opener at the shelf behind the desk.

'Thanks,' she said, stretching across the desk.

He hadn't thought it through.

A whisper of warmth feathered his cheek as the edge of the white coat caught on his chair and then she put her hand on his shoulder to steady herself as she wobbled on those ridiculous heels.

'Oops…'

'Can you reach?'

'I've got it. Thanks.'

He waited, holding his breath, willing her to move but, having found what she was looking for, she remained where she was, apparently transfixed by the invoices piling up in front of him.

'Are those all unpaid bills?' she asked, horrified.

He removed another final demand from its envelope and placed it on one of three piles. 'It's not quite as bad as it looks,' he said.

'It isn't?'

She smelt amazing. Warm skin, clean hair mingled with starched white cotton, vanilla, chocolate… Something else… He struggled against the urge to turn and pull her close, bury his face against the silk and breathe deeper. Effort wasted as she bent over his shoulder to take a closer look at the bills. Sun-warmed strawberries. That was it. Not raspberries, but strawberries. One of those dark red varieties, full of flavour, dripping with juice that would stain her mouth…

'I'm using a triage system,' he said, desperate for any distraction from thoughts of hot, juice-stained lips… 'Those on the left are the original invoices, the ones in the middle are reminders and these…' he tapped the pile with the letter opener; he needed to do something with his hands '…are final demands.'

'Oh, dear God. Poor Ria.' The strappy thing she was wearing fell away as she bent to pick up the electricity bill, offering him a glimpse of softly mounded breasts in creamy lace cups. Had she no control over her clothing? Shouldn't she have buttoned up the white coat?

There had to be rules…

'Praying won't help,' he said, even as he offered up a God-help-me on his own account, 'but the telephone has already been cut off so I suggest you get cracking on your sorbet before the electricity company follows suit.'

His attempt to send her scurrying back to the prep room failed. 'I'll go across to the bank and pay it now.'

'Why would you do that?' he asked, making the mistake of looking up and discovering that her lips were barely a breath away from his own.

Ripe, red, sweet...

For a moment her eyes, misty green beneath long dark lashes, connected with his and a fizz of heat went straight to his groin as the air filled with pheromones. His reaction must have telegraphed itself to her because, with a tiny hiss of breath, she straightened, took half a step back.

It wasn't the reaction he had expected. He'd assumed that getting close was part of her plan, but apparently he'd misread her and now he was the one being tormented by X-rated images of those long legs, that hot body and sweet strawberry lips...

'Because I can? You can deduct it from the rent,' she said, recovering before him.

'Nice try, but then the business will owe you money.'

'As well as ice cream. I know, but I can't run the business without electricity, Mr West. Or did you really think I was just stringing you along until I'd finished this order?'

'It had crossed my mind,' he said abruptly, plucking the invoice from her hand and returning it to the pile.

'Well, uncross it. I've got another business function next week,' she said, the sharpness of her voice undermined by the faintest wobble on the word 'function'. Despite her swift move out of the danger zone, the heat had not been all one way. The thought that she might be suffering too went some small way to easing his own discomfort...

'Another function?'

'You needn't sound so surprised,' she said. 'A local company holding a gala dinner has commissioned us to provide miniature ice-cream cones late in the evening. When everyone is hot from dancing,' she added, presumably in case he didn't get it.

He got it. He was hot…

'I'll rephrase that,' he said. 'I was *hoping* that you were stringing me along until you finished this order. That this was a one off.'

'You didn't believe I was serious? About making an offer for the business?'

'Not for a minute.'

Her forehead buckled in the faintest of frowns as if she couldn't understand why he wasn't taking her seriously. Maybe he was underestimating her. Judging her on appearance. Or just plain distracted by the flash-over of heat whenever they came within touching distance.

'I've got events booked throughout the summer, Mr West. Weddings, hen parties, business parties. They must be in Ria's diary.'

'Ria and her diary are no longer in the ice-cream business so you'd better find another supplier or come up with an offer very quickly,' he replied.

'I will. Just as soon as I've seen the accounts.' He waited for her to flounce out of the room. She didn't. Flounce, bounce or depart with the kind of door-banging pique warranted by the way he'd spoken to her. Instead she continued to regard him with that slightly puzzled frown. 'You must realise that it's in your best interests to sell the business as a going concern.'

'Must I?'

Her throat moved as she swallowed.

She might be sticking to her guns, no matter what he threw at her, but she was nowhere near as composed as she would have him believe. What would she do if he looped his arm around her waist, pulled her down onto his lap and let her feel just how discomposed he was?

'You could keep Nancy on to run the ice-cream parlour,' she suggested, when he offered no encouragement. 'That way money will still be coming in and there's more likelihood that the creditors will be paid. And the business will be worth more to any buyer.'

'That it would be in your best interests, I have no doubt,' he replied as the ground beneath him shifted, sucked him in.

What would she do if he slid his hands beneath that scrap of cloth masquerading as a skirt and lifted her onto the desk?

'Hardly.' She leaned back, her bottom propped on the desk, almost as if she could read his mind, were inviting him to run his hand up the inside of her thigh... 'I could wait until you're selling up, buy the equipment and freezers at a knock-down price and rent a unit near my office.'

'You'd lose the ice-cream parlour,' he said, not sure why he was even wasting his time discussing it with her. Except that it kept her beside him, touching close.

'That's the upside,' she pointed out, with a gesture that lifted her skirt another inch. 'I have no use for a retail outlet.'

'And the downside?'

All he had to do was move his chair a few inches, slip his hand inside the starchy white coat, under her skirt and his hands would be cradling that peachy backside...

'I'd have to start from scratch...' her voice faded to fragments '...take time...transport problem...'

...fill his mouth with the taste of ripe strawberries and honey...

'And it would be difficult for Nancy to get to Haughton Manor on the bus.'

Haughton Manor?

So, she was the offspring of minor gentry. No surprise there. The sexy clothes, the casual attitude, the silly ice creams were all the marks of a woman playing at business until the right man came along. One who could support her shoe habit.

And he was reacting exactly like his father. A man who'd used his wealth and position to indulge his love of bright, shiny things. Cars, boats, women...

See it, want it, discard it when the novelty wore off...

It was a thought as chilling as a cold shower on a January morning.

CHAPTER FIVE

Never send to know for whom the ice cream bell chimes;
it chimes for thee!
—*from Rosie's 'Little Book of Ice Cream'*

'YOU SHOULDN'T BE telling me that,' Alexander said, telling himself that he didn't give a hoot who or what she was. Or her business. And as for Nancy, he'd paid her off...

Just like your father...

The words dropped into his head like lead weight, but what else could he do? He'd made sure she had enough money to tide her over until she found another job.

And if she didn't...?

'Why?' Sorrel demanded, reclaiming his attention. She was clearly perplexed by his attitude. 'Do you think you're going to be trampled in the crush to buy an ice-cream parlour?'

'No. But then I'm not interested in selling.'

'What about Ria? What will she do if this place closes? You're the one who suggested I offer her a job.'

'I also told you she wouldn't take it.'

'Why not? I'd take care of the paperwork leaving her to concentrate on the ice cream. She'd have all the fun and none of the worry.'

If that was supposed to reassure him, to have him over-come with gratitude, she had misjudged his gullibility by a factor of ten. But then he knew Ria a lot better than she did. And he knew nothing about Sorrel Amery, except that she'd sent his hormones into meltdown. But while his body might be ready to leap blindly into bed with her, he wasn't about to let his libido make business decisions.

'I didn't realise that ice cream had become such an essential ingredient in corporate entertaining,' he said, and if he sounded as sceptical as he felt it was intentional.

'It's not. Yet. But I'm getting there,' she assured him.

'Frankly, I'm amazed it's happening at all.'

'Yes, your amazement is coming through loud and clear, Mr West—'

'Alexander,' he said, irritably. His father had been Mr West. 'Alexander…'

His name was soft on her tongue. Like a lover's whisper in his ear and he wished he'd let it go. 'Mr West' was safer. A lot safer.

'Maybe you should come along to an event and see for yourself how we do it,' she suggested, rather more crisply as she gave him an assessing once-over. 'Get a haircut and if you've got a dinner jacket, I'll give you a job, too. I can always use a good-looking waiter.'

He resisted the urge to rake his fingers through his hair, grab an elastic band from the pot on the desk and fasten it back. 'I'll pass, thanks all the same.' She didn't move. 'I thought you were in a hurry to track down Nancy,' he said, willing her to leave.

'I am, but…'

'What?'

'Your, um, amazement must be catching,' she said. 'Cutting off the electricity would be a very simple way of getting rid of me.'

Apparently she didn't trust him any more than he trusted

her. Clearly she was smarter than she looked. But not that smart.

'It would. Unfortunately, with freezers filled with Knickerbocker Gloria's only asset, securing the electricity supply is top of my list.'

'Is it?' she asked, clearly puzzled. 'I would have thought the cost of one would have offset the other. Ria makes fresh ices three times a week for the ice-cream parlour, so there can't be that much stock. In your shoes I'd have flushed the lot down the sink.'

Okay. She *was* that smart.

'The bill will have to be paid sooner or later.' His brain cocked a sceptical eye at him as he took out his wallet and, using his mobile phone, called the number on the final demand, tapping in the details of his debit card in response to the prompts. 'I'm taking the sooner option.'

He wrote 'paid', the time, date and card he'd used on the invoice before tossing it on top of the tax account in the 'out' tray. He saw her raised eyebrows and said, 'Okay, the electric bill was my number two priority. With fines by the day, paying the Revenue had to be number one.'

'Good decision,' she said. The thoughtful look she gave him said a lot more, but he wanted Sorrel with her luscious mouth, chestnut hair and endless legs out of his space before he consigned his brain to the devil and let his body do the thinking.

'If you're feeling grateful, the coffee pot is empty,' he said. 'And if you're going out to stock up on champagne and cucumbers, you can bring me back a bacon roll.'

'Does Ria run errands for you?'

'Landlord's perks.'

'Don't bank on getting them from me,' she said, making it clear she thought that they amounted to more than sandwiches.

'Not one created out of ice cream,' he warned, 'but hot, from the baker on the corner. Heavy on the brown sauce.'

* * *

Nancy's phone went straight to voicemail and Sorrel left a message asking her to call back as a matter of urgency. She'd already tried Ria's mobile and got a message saying that the number was not available, which was worrying. If she'd cut all her ties…

No. Alexander had said she was safe. Presumably he had a contact number even if he wasn't prepared to share. She wished she'd taken more notice when Ria talked about her friends in Wales. She'd sent a card the last time. She still had it somewhere…

Meanwhile, she cleaned out the coffee maker and refilled it.

Alexander West might have set her nerves jangling, disturbing her more than any man she'd ever met—irritating her, with his dismissal of her ability to run a business based on nothing but the length of her skirt—but a pot of coffee was a small price to pay for the lifeline he had, no matter how reluctantly, thrown her.

He didn't acknowledge her as she plugged it back in and switched it on. His attention was focused on the computer screen and since he was probably trying to work out where all the money had gone—and how much he could persuade her to pay for the business—she did not disturb him.

There was only so much 'amazement' a woman could take in one day.

She rubbed the back of her hand over her mouth as if to erase the memory of his kiss. It only brought the moment more vividly to life and he hadn't even been trying. If he'd followed through on the heat that had come off him like an oven door opening as he'd turned to look up at her…

No.

Absolutely not.

He was just passing through and she didn't do one-night,

or even one-week stands. It had been a very long time since she'd even come close. Graeme…

She shook her head. Their relationship wasn't about sex, it was about partnership. Their marriage, when it happened, would be based on mutual respect and support. Built to last. Not some flash-in-the-pan, here today, gone tomorrow, lust-driven madness.

Right now, her sole focus was her business; making it a household name in the events world.

She fetched her laptop from the van, checked the recipes Ria had given her, listed what she'd need to make the missing ices, but she couldn't stop thinking about the sudden collapse of Ria's business and Alexander West's involvement in it all.

He was certainly not the freeloader she'd thought him. He'd put his hand in his own pocket to pay a couple of hefty bills—and not, apparently, for the first time.

Whatever his relationship with Ria, it went deep. And was, she reminded herself for the umpteenth time, none of her business.

Really.

She did need to speak to Ria, though, and tried her home number. Her call went straight to voicemail. She left a message promising to help, urging her to come back. There was nothing in her own message box that wouldn't wait but, seeking a little steadiness to counteract the last couple of hours, she returned a call from Graeme Laing. He was not only her financial advisor and mentor since university, but everything she'd ever wanted in a man.

'Sorrel… Thanks for getting back to me so quickly.' Calm, ordered—at the sound of his voice, her pulse rate immediately began to settle. 'I've managed to get tickets for the gala opening of La Bohème and I need to know if you'll be free on the twenty-fourth.'

'Really?' She tried to sound excited. 'I thought they were like gold dust.'

'They are. Someone owed me a favour.' No surprise there. He was the kind of man everyone wanted on their side in the turbulent financial world. Picking up on her lack of enthusiasm, he said, 'Puccini is at the lighter end of the operatic scale, Sorrel. You'll enjoy it.'

'Only one person dies?' she said, half jokingly. The closest she'd ever wanted to get to an opera involved a Phantom and her pulse rate was now non-existent.

'This is grand opera,' he said, a touch impatiently—he didn't joke about the 'arts', 'not a soap opera.'

'I read that the soap writers trawl Greek tragedies for their plot ideas.'

'Really?' he replied, with about as much enthusiasm for the idea as hers for a night at the opera. Graeme might have said that she was everything he'd ever want in a wife but she was, no question, still a work in progress. Her sisters weren't entirely kidding when they referred to him as 'Professor Higgins'.

It wasn't like that. Well, not totally like that. Any man would want his wife to enjoy his passions and she'd always known exactly what she wanted in a man. Graeme was her perfect fit and she would do her best to be his. On the bright side she could wear the vintage Schiaparelli gown she'd found at the back of a junk shop a couple of months ago. It was perfect for mingling with millionaires at the post-gala party because it wasn't about opera, it was about networking. Being seen with the right people, being noticed and it was the world she had aspired to since she'd chosen a business rather than an academic career. When she was a millionaire, no one would care who her mother was, or think her beneath them.

'It'll be fun,' she said, doing her best to sound more enthusiastic. You didn't get anything worthwhile without a little suffering and it could be worse. Much worse. Graeme could have been a cricket fanatic—a game that involved entire days of boredom. 'Remind me when it is? I'll have to call you back when I've checked my diary. With Elle on maternity leave I'm filling in with Rosie as well as the big events.' At least he understood that business took priority over everything. Even death by singing. 'Right now I've got a bit of a crisis on the ice-cream front.'

'What's that woman done now?' And the opera was forgotten as they returned to familiar, if contentious, territory. Ria was definitely not his idea of a businesswoman. Perfect or otherwise.

'Are you free this evening?' she asked, avoiding the question. 'I need to talk to you about the possibility of raising some finance.'

'Finance? I thought I'd made it plain that you need to consolidate before thinking about taking any more risks. Next year, maybe.'

'Yes, yes…' he'd been saying that for the last two years and at this rate she'd be fifty-five before she achieved her ambition '…but it's a matter of adapting to circumstances.' Quoting one of his favourite axioms back at him. 'I want to make an offer for Knickerbocker Gloria.'

'She's in trouble?' he asked, with what sounded like the smallest touch of self-satisfied 'I told you so' *Schadenfreude*. 'Well, you know what I think.' The free-spirited, disorganised Ria and the intensely focused, totally organised Graeme were never going to find common ground. 'Don't let sentiment jump you into doing anything hasty.'

'I won't,' she assured him, 'but I don't have time to talk right now,' she said, irritated that he felt he had to remind her of business basics. She was grateful for his support, his advice, but this wasn't about profit and loss. This was about something much more important. Friendship. The future. Magic.

Ideas were going off like rockets in her head and the minute she'd dealt with the immediate crisis, she'd put them down on paper. Prepare a business plan. If she could show him the money, he'd listen.

'Leave it with me. This might well play into our hands. I'll make some enquiries, find out exactly how much trouble she's in—'

'I appreciate the offer, Graeme, but to be honest if you have that much free time, I could do with a hand mixing up a batch of cucumber ice cream,' she said, unable to resist a little payback for his smug satisfaction that he'd been proved right about Ria.

'Won't I need a hygiene certificate?'

'Any excuse,' she said, unable to stop herself from laughing out loud. He was so predictable!

'Oh, you were joking.'

'There is absolutely nothing funny about ice cream, Graeme,' she said, mentally slapping her wrist for teasing him, but doing it anyway. 'I'll have to arrange a training session for you with the catering students at the local college.'

'I'm more use to you on the financial front,' he replied, seriously. 'I'll find out what I can about the financial state of Knickerbocker Gloria so that we can make the best of the situation.' We... That implied it would be the two of them. Working together. So long as she agreed with him. The thought popped, unbidden, into her head. 'You'll let me know whether you'll be free on the twenty-fourth?'

'The twenty-fourth.' She made a note. 'I'll call you this evening.'

She cut the connection wishing she hadn't said anything about Ria's financial problem. Obviously she needed information, but she hated the thought of him poking around in

Ria's problems, knowing that he'd put the worst possible slant on things.

Which was stupid. There was no room for sentiment in business and obviously she couldn't go into this blind. He was right about that. That was *why* she always agreed with him, because he was right about everything.

Graeme was her rock, she reminded herself. He might not make her heart race, or her head swim the way Alexander West had done with nothing more than a look, the lightest of touches, a kiss that had made her toes curl. Okay, so maybe he did have a bit of a sense of humour bypass, but he was utterly dependable and that was worth a heck of a lot more than a momentary sizzle on the lips.

When she returned with everything she needed to finish the Jefferson order, there was no sign of Nancy and she still wasn't answering her phone so as soon as she'd unloaded the van, Sorrel went to the baker's.

She wouldn't, ever, run 'errands' for any man with two sound legs but the artisan baker on the corner supplied custommade baked goods for Scoop! and she had to pick up some more items for the Jefferson order. Since she'd had a very early start herself with no sign of a lunch break in the foreseeable future, she bought herself a sandwich while she was about it.

'Here's your bacon roll, Alex...' Her voice died away as she saw him, head on his arms, fast asleep on Ria's desk.

His shoulders appeared to be even wider spread across the desk, his back impossibly broad. His glossy hair had slipped over his face, leaving just a glimpse of a strong jaw and chin, the stubble of a man who hadn't bothered to shave that morning throwing the sensuous curve of his mouth into stark relief. Even the thought of running her fingertips over his cheek triggered a prickle of awareness, a melting heat, shocking in its intimacy.

'Memo to self,' she murmured under her breath as she stepped back, away from temptation. 'Make the coffee stronger.'

'Thanks for the roll.'

Sorrel, whizzing up cucumbers in the blender, jumped as Alexander turned on the tap and rinsed out his mug before upending it on the draining board.

'No problem.' She glanced sideways at him. His cheek was slightly pink and crumpled where his head had been resting on his arm and there was a deep red imprint on his face where the heavy winder of his wristwatch had dug in. It was an old steel Rolex very like the one her grandfather had worn and which Elle had sold, along with anything else of value her family had owned.

The con man who'd left them destitute had been too smart to steal anything physical, but it had all gone anyway. First he'd stolen their security. Then their family history written in the marks on the Sheraton dining table where generations had propped their elbows, the Georgian silver brought out for celebrations, the wear on a carpet her great-grandfather had brought back from Persia. Along with the jewellery, no more than a glittering memory in old photographs, and the precious things collected over two centuries, it had all gone to the salesrooms to pay off the overdraft, the credit cards he'd applied for in their grandmother's name. Fraud, of course, but she had signed the forms...

'Feeling better after your nap?' she asked.

It came out rather more snarkily than she'd intended but she should be at Cranbrook, checking that everything was in place in the Conservatory for tomorrow, instead of here, putting cucumbers through a blender.

Not his fault, she reminded herself.

'Marginally.' Muscles rippled under his T-shirt as he rotated his right shoulder to ease the muscles. 'It's going to take a couple of days for my body to catch up with this time zone.'

'Really?' Her mouth was unaccountably dry. She ran her tongue over her teeth, a trick Graeme had told her was used by nervous speakers to help her with early client presentations. 'What time zone is your body loitering in?'

Well, it would have been rude not to ask.

'Somewhere around the international date line,' he said. 'On an island you won't have heard of.'

'One with long white beaches, coconut-shell cocktails and dusky maidens in grass skirts?' she suggested. Well, she'd seen the postcards. 'Far too many distractions to waste time writing home, obviously.'

'Thick jungle. Mosquitoes as big as bats, bats as big as cats,' he countered, 'and no corner shops selling postcards or stamps.'

'Well, that doesn't sound like much fun,' she replied, covering her surprise pretty well, considering. Because it didn't. Sound like fun. 'You need to have a serious talk with your travel agent.'

'I don't think Pantabalik has made it onto this year's must-visit list of tourist venues.'

'I can see why,' she said, her irritation evaporating in the unexpected warmth of his smile. Apparently 'exploring' wasn't, as she'd assumed, a euphemism for living the life of a lotus-eater, but something rather more taxing. 'So where did that last postcard come from?'

'An airport transit lounge.'

'You have been having a bad time. Maybe you should give your body a break and go home to bed.'

'Thanks for your concern, but my body is used to surviving on catnaps.' He rotated his left shoulder.

'Don't...' The word slipped out.

'What?'

'Do that.' The tongue-teeth thing was working overtime. 'Your T-shirt won't stand the strain.'

Forget his T-shirt, it was her blood pressure that was about to blow…

He turned his head and looked down at his shoulder, poking at the split with his finger, and shrugged. 'Sweat rots the cotton.'

'Too much information,' she said, tearing her eyes away as the gap lengthened, grabbing the heavy jug of puréed cucumber to mix it with measured amounts of crème fraîche, lime juice and salt.

She needed two hands to lift it and he said, 'Let me do that.'

She didn't argue as he took it from her, not meeting his eyes as she stepped back out of the forbidden zone of warm male flesh, disintegrating clothing, a ripple of heat that lapped against her, disturbing the order of the universe whenever he was too close.

'Thank you,' she said, concentrating very hard on the mixture, determined to block out the thought of him sliding naked between Ria's lavender-scented sheets, only to be assailed by the image of him stretched out in a hammock slung between trees hung with lianas, his golden body glistening with sweat beneath a gauzy mosquito net…

Whatever was the matter with her?

Her universe was fixed. Centred. Planned out to the last detail. For the moment her focus was Scoop! In a year or two she'd marry Graeme in the village church, live in the Georgian rectory next door that he'd recently bought. It would take that long to renovate it to his exacting standards. Which not only covered stationary but signalled his intention of settling down in the vicinity of her office, her family. It was solid, real…

'I wouldn't sleep much with oversized mosquitoes and bats flying around, either,' she said. Concentrate on the bats… 'What were you doing there? In Pan…?'

'Pantabalik.'

'Pantabalik. You're right,' she said. 'I've never heard of it.' She glanced at him. Geography was a safe subject.

'I was on a plant-hunting expedition.'

'Plant hunting?' she repeated, startled. 'How very...'

Unlikely... Unpredictable... Unexpected...

'How very what?' His eyebrows invited all kinds of indiscretions.

'How very Victorian,' she said, primly, turning off the machine and, reaching for a plastic spoon from a pot on the work surface, she dipped it into the mixture and tasted it. Creamy, with a big hit of cucumber, but something was missing... 'I have this image of you wearing a pith helmet as you hack your way through the undergrowth hunting for a fabled species of orchid.'

'A hat is essential. You never know what is going to fall out of a tree.' She glanced up and saw the betraying kink in the corner of his mouth. Felt a responding flutter... 'Personally I favour a wide-brimmed Akubra, but each to his own.'

Oh, yes. She could see him in something wide-brimmed and battered from hard wear... 'And the orchid?' she asked.

'Sorry. Not my thing.'

She shrugged. 'Shame. There's something so erotic about orchids...'

Exotic... She'd meant to say 'exotic', but correcting herself would only draw attention to the word and make things ten times worse. Turning quickly back to the mixture before he could say something outrageous, she changed the subject.

'I followed the recipe Ria used for the original, but she must have added something else to the sample she gave me to take to Jefferson's.'

'The magic.'

'Yes...' She sighed. 'Unfortunately I don't have a wand to

wave over it, so if you have something a little more tangible in the way of suggestion I'd be grateful.'

'Does it matter? I mean, who's tasted it besides you and someone in Jefferson's marketing department?'

'Actually, it was Nick's wife who tasted the ices and made the final selection.'

'In that case you are in trouble.'

'No question.' Nick Jefferson was married to Cassie Cornwell, the famous television cook, and she'd certainly notice that something was missing. 'And even if it hadn't been someone who knew the difference, this is not what I promised them.' She took another spoon from the pot and scooped up a little. 'Any ideas?' she asked, offering it to him.

CHAPTER SIX

A balanced diet is an ice cream in each hand.
—from Rosie's 'Little Book of Ice Cream'

SORREL HAD ASSUMED Alexander would take the spoon from her but instead he leaned forward and put his lips around it. His hair fell forward and brushed against her wrist, goosing her flesh, and he put his hand beneath hers to steady it when it began to shake. Then he raised heavy lids to look straight into her eyes.

They were dangerously close.

It was a rerun of that moment when he'd been opening Ria's bills. He'd turned to look at her then and the down on her cheek had stirred as if he had touched her, the effect rippling through her body in ever widening circles, like a pebble dropped into still water. It was utterly physical, her body bypassing the brain, whispering seductively, *'Forget safe, forget dependable. Forget Graeme...'*

She'd taken an involuntary step back, shocked by such a powerful response to a man whom, while undeniably attractive, she was not predisposed to like. But lust had nothing to do with liking. It was an unthinking, mindless, live-now-pay-later physical response to the atavistic need of a species to reproduce itself. A lingering madness, as outdated, as unnecessary, as troublesome as the appendix. It meant nothing.

And yet, with his palm cradling her hand, face-to-face, the effect was amplified; not so much a ripple as a tsunami…

Even as she floundered, out of her depth, going under, he released her hand, turned away, reached for his mug and filled it from the tap.

That was what she needed, too. Water. Lots and lots of cold water…

She had to settle for drawing in a deep, slightly ragged breath while his back was turned.

'Was it that bad?' she asked, needing to say something, pretend that nothing had happened. His throat rippled disturbingly as he drained the water and she swallowed, too. 'The ice cream?'

He glanced at her, then at the cup. Shook his head. 'No. Not at all. You just have to get past the expectation that it will be sweet.' He appeared to be completely unaware of the effect he'd had on her, thank goodness. 'How are you serving it?' He nodded towards the ice cream.

'Oh… A teaspoonful squished between tiny triangle-shaped oatmeal biscuits so that it looks like a miniature sandwich.' He pulled a face, unimpressed. She began to breathe more easily. 'You don't approve?'

'I've tasted some oatmeal biscuits that closely resembled cardboard.'

'These won't.' And gradually she eased back out of the quicksand of feelings running out of control, climbing back onto the firmer ground of the stuff she understood. 'I picked them up this morning along with your bacon roll. Peter produces all our baked goods. Biscuits, tuiles, brandy snaps.'

'Our?'

'Scoop! is a family business. My older sister started it with the unexpected gift of a vintage ice-cream van. My younger sister—the animal lover—is an art student. She does the artwork for the PR and runs the website.'

It was probably best not to mention her grandmother, who helped style their events, or her great-uncle Basil, a fabulous maître d' at the big events and, when called upon, happy to don a striped blazer and straw boater to do a turn for them on an ancient ice-cream bicycle that he had lovingly restored.

'And you?' he asked. 'What do you do?'

'Me?' She was the one who was going to turn their brand into a household name but she decided that, rather like the extended family, in this instance it was an ambition better kept private. Alexander's eyebrow, like her pulse rate, had been given more than enough exercise for one day. 'I'm the one who's stuck here making ice cream when I should be in the newly restored Victorian Conservatory at Cranbrook Park, ensuring that the ice-cream bar is installed and fully functioning and that everything is in place for a perfect event.' The eyebrow barely twitched. 'Meanwhile, for your information, the biscuit we chose bears no resemblance to cardboard but is a thin, crisp, melt-in-the-mouth savoury oatmeal shortbread.'

'If Peter Sands baked it, I'm warming to the idea.'

'You know Peter?'

'I wouldn't have a bacon roll from anyone else.'

'Great,' she said, not sure whether he was serious, or simply winding her up. The latter, she feared. Unless... 'You're his landlord, too, aren't you?'

'I am, but I don't sleep with him, either,' he said. 'In case you were wondering.'

'No.' She wasn't wondering that. Not at all. 'As for the florist, the delicatessen and the haberdashery in between...'

He shifted, as if she'd caught him off guard, and suddenly everything clicked into place. It wasn't just this corner. The entire area had been given a makeover three or four years ago. Cleaned up, refreshed, while still keeping its old-fashioned charm.

'Ohmigod! You're *that* West!'

'No,' he said, waiting for her to catch up. '*That* West died in nineteen forty-one.'

'You know what I mean,' she said, crossly. Maybridge had been little more than a village that had grown up around a toll bridge when James West had started manufacturing his 'liver pills' in a cottage on the other side of the river. The gothic mansion built in the nineteenth century on the hill overlooking the town by one of Alexander's ancestors was now the headquarters of the multinational West Pharmaceutical Group. 'Your family built this town. Could I feel any more stupid?'

'Why? The name was dropped from the company after some scandal involving my great-great-grandfather and a married woman. You could stop a hundred people in the town and not one of them would know that the W in WPG stands for West.'

'Maybe, but I did,' she admitted. How could she not have made the connection? Too many other things on her mind... 'I did a project on the town history for my GCSE. I got in touch with their marketing department and they gave me a tour of the place.' She shivered. 'All that marble and mahogany.'

'And the building is listed so they can't rip it out.' It appeared to amuse him.

'They have close links with the university, too. Research, recruitment.'

'They're proactive when it comes to headhunting for talent.'

'I know.' She was going to enjoy this next bit... 'They offered me a place in their management scheme.'

'And you turned it down?' He sounded sceptical. Unsurprising, if rude. No one turned down an offer from WPG. But no one else had Scoop!

'Why would I want to sit in the office of some giant corporation, moving figures around, when I could be dreaming up ways to make someone's day with the perfect ice cream?' She regarded him thoughtfully. 'I'd have thought a man who chose mosquitoes and bats over the boardroom would have understood that.'

'Touché.' He grinned appreciatively and she responded with a little curtsey.

'Sadly, I don't have the rents from half Maybridge to support my lifestyle.'

'Who does? While my great-great-grandfather built this end of the High Street, his property portfolio, like WPG, is run by a charitable trust.'

'So you're not Ria's landlord.'

'I sit on the board of trustees.'

'Which no doubt philanthropically supports your plant-hunting expeditions?'

'All plant hunters need a patron with deep pockets. They do reap the benefits from my finds.'

'So, what do you get out of it, apart from mosquito bites?' she asked.

'The glory?' he suggested. 'The fun?'

Which pretty much told her everything she needed to know about Alexander West. She might have got the wrong end of the stick when it came to his relationship with Ria, but she'd had him nailed from the start.

'If fun's your thing,' she said, grabbing the opportunity to score another point, 'you should have been at the Christmas party WPG threw at the children's hospice in Melchester last year. They booked Rosie and we decked her out as Santa's sleigh, flying in from the North Pole with ices for everyone.'

'With you as Santa's Little Helper, no doubt.'

'Actually I was the ice-cream fairy.' There was no point in denying her involvement, there was photographic evidence on their blog. There was no reason why he would bother to look up Scoop!, but it paid to cover all contingencies. 'My sister was pregnant at the time so she couldn't fit into the costume.'

He grinned. 'I'm sorry I missed it.'

'Me, too. You wouldn't be giving me so much grief about our competence. Meanwhile, time is short. Would you care to venture an opinion on whether this recipe needs more lime, or a little mint perhaps?' she asked, clutching at straws as she tried to recall the exact taste of the ice cream they had sampled in Cassie's kitchen. Work out what 'magic' ingredient Ria might have added when she'd prepared the tasting samples.

'Neither.'

He took the spoon she was still holding, turned it over and pulled it through his lips, sucking off every last trace of ice in a deliberately provocative manner. Or maybe she was reading things into his actions that she wanted to be there.

No, no, no! What was she thinking?

She resisted the urge to fan herself as he leaned back against the sink, tapping the spoon against that seductive lower lip, and thought for a moment.

Provocation was the last thing she needed...

'What it needs,' he said, after what seemed like an age while she held her breath, 'is a touch of cayenne pepper.'

'Cayenne?' The word came out in a rush of breath. She knew all about chocolate and chilli—she and Ria had been working on that for their next event—but no... 'A cucumber sandwich is supposed to be cool. The epitome of English sangfroid.'

The very opposite of what she was feeling right now.

'You asked. That's my opinion.' He tossed the spoon in the bin, clearly not bothered one way or the other whether she took his advice. 'I imagine you've tried calling Ria?'

'Yes, of course. It was the first thing I did. Her mobile is unavailable. I'm assuming she's switched off to avoid being hounded by creditors.'

'Is that what you'd do?'

'Me? I'd never let things get to this point.'

'Never say never.'

'I don't suppose you know of any other number she uses?' she asked, refusing to rise to this new provocation. He had no way of knowing why she would never let that happen and she certainly wasn't about to tell him. 'I keep a separate phone for personal calls.'

'You have that many?'

'It's just more professional,' she replied, leaving the number of calls she received to his imagination. Although come to think of it Graeme didn't seem to get it, either. He always called her on her business number, even when he had tickets for the hottest opera in town. Was that how he saw her? Even now? She wasn't the only young entrepreneur he helped. But she was the only one he took to dinners, social functions. The damned opera.

Until today that hadn't seemed important. On the contrary. It was the perfect partnership. He was the perfect date. Elegant, intelligent and undemanding. She appeared to be his. Well dressed, intelligent—and undemanding.

It had seemed perfect, but suddenly a vast, empty space yawned in the centre of their relationship. Would Graeme drop everything and travel halfway across the world if she needed him?

'No one could ever accuse Ria of being professional.' Alexander's voice broke into her thoughts.

'No.' That was the point: Graeme wouldn't have to cross continents. He'd be there. She shook her head to clear it. 'No,' she repeated. 'I've only seen her with an old BlackBerry,' she said, catching up. It didn't rule out the possibility that she had another phone, of course. One that was kept for special calls.

Just because Alexander's postcards were a rare event, it didn't mean that they didn't talk to one another when he was lying in his jungle hammock.

It was a thought that jarred, although… 'How did you manage to receive a call from her, if you were in a mosquito-infested jungle?' she asked.

'Despite my Victorian occupation, I have a twenty-first-century satellite link to keep in touch with the outside world. But to answer your question, Ria has never mentioned another number to me. I was rather hoping you might know of one. She did trust you with a key.'

'She trusts you with her bank account.'

'It was a condition of bailing her out last time.' He put the cup in the sink. 'Maybe Nancy can tell you what the magic ingredient is.'

'I'm not having much luck with phones today. Her number went straight to voicemail, too.' Which was odd. She wouldn't have switched it off if she was job-hunting. 'Maybe the battery's flat.' It was that kind of day. 'I've left a message but if she hasn't called me back by three I'll go along to the school and catch her there. You've no objection if I ask her to come in to work tomorrow?'

'Would it make any difference if I had?' She didn't bother to answer that. 'I thought not.' He shrugged. 'You can ask but you'll have to pay her.'

'Friday is a busy day,' she pointed out, 'and we've been promised a heatwave for the weekend. You'll shift a lot of ice cream. If you talked to the Revenue, explain that you've got someone interested…'

'Forget it. I'll be talking to the bank and Ria's accountant about winding up the business.'

'Actually, I don't think you'll find him at his office. I'm sure Ria mentioned that he'd been taken ill. A stroke, I think. So that's one thing you can cross off your list.'

'He has a partner.'

'Selling ice cream is a lot more fun,' she assured him. 'Really.'

'Maybe, but I didn't fly halfway around the world to stand behind an ice-cream counter.'

Which begged the question, why exactly had he flown halfway round the world? It was none of her business. At all.

'Okay,' she said, with what she hoped looked like a careless shrug, 'if I can't tempt you, I'll pay Nancy, but I'm not a charity. If I'm paying rent for the premises and paying the staff, I'll buy the ice cream and bank the takings.'

That raised a smile. 'The first sensible thing you've said today.'

Actually, it wasn't. Ria might have the magic touch with ice cream, but she was the one with an instinct for business. Her offer to buy Knickerbocker Gloria might have been a throwaway remark but, the more she thought about it, the more excited she became.

It had been her sister who, without any business experience, had seen an opportunity and changed their lives. They'd all helped—she'd been the one who knew about regulations, accounting procedures, tax—but it was Elle who had seized the moment. Suddenly she was having a 'big idea' of her own. Maybe *the* 'big idea'.

She was shaking a little as she grinned back at Alexander. 'I'm glad you approve. So, do we have a deal, Alexander West?'

'If you can pay a month's rent in advance, Sorrel Amery.'

'A month?'

'It'll take that long to prepare the accounts, negotiate a new lease with the trust, contracts. Take it or leave it.'

She shrugged. 'I don't seem to have much choice. How much are you going to charge me?' she asked. He wasn't the only one who could ask a 'catch' question. She knew exactly how much rent Ria paid.

He didn't ask for a penny more.

'Will that be in cash?' She was pushing her luck, but she

didn't want him to know that a month suited her very well. She needed time. 'Without the telephone you won't be able to use the card machine.'

'A cheque would be tidier. Make it payable to The WPG Trust.' Then, as if it had just occurred to him, he said, 'Oh, no. You don't carry a cheque book with you.'

He was *teasing* her?

She opened her bag. 'Oh, look,' she said, producing it. 'This must be your lucky day.'

'You think?'

The teasing glint remained, but realising how much trouble Ria was causing him, how much trouble *she* was causing him, she said, 'No. I'm sorry.' Then, because this was business, 'My cheque for one month's rent to be refunded off the price if I make an offer for the business?' she pressed, firmly repressing the whisper of longing that shimmered through her as the suggestion of a smile, lifting one corner of his mouth, deepened a little.

'To be refunded off the price if you buy the business,' he agreed and offered her his hand. It was one of the traditional ways to close a deal. A kiss was another.

Kissing him would be fun.

Glorious fun...

For heaven's sake! This was serious!

She grasped his hand firmly, like a proper business person. It was hard, callused, vibrating with power and this was him with jet lag...

'I imagine you'll want that in writing?' he asked, losing the smile and releasing her so abruptly that she practically fell off her heels.

She took half a step back to regain her balance, physical if not mental. 'What do you think?'

'I think you should put some cayenne pepper in that ice cream,' he said, peeling himself away from the sink.

The air seemed to ripple around him as he moved, lapping against her in soft waves, goosing her flesh. Sorrel shivered a little and glanced after him. Did he have that effect on everyone or was it just her?

He didn't look back, and, aware that she was standing there in a lustlorn trance, she was grateful. The click of the door as he closed it brought her back to reality, but even then it took a moment for her bones to remember what they were for. What she was here for.

Cayenne pepper? Really?

She crossed the kitchen and opened the cupboard containing the spice and flavourings and there it was. Right at the front.

Could he be right?

In the face of any other ideas it had to be worth a try, but how much was just a touch, exactly? She liked everything cut and dried. Laid out in straight lines. Business, life, gram weights. Give her a recipe and she was fine but this 'touch', or 'pinch' business—like the sizzle in the air whenever they came within touching distance—left her floundering.

She weighed some of the spice carefully onto the little 'gram' scale and then added it to a pint of the mixture in the tiniest amounts, tasting, adding, tasting, adding until suddenly the ice cream sprang to life. Not hot, but with just enough added zing to make it…perfect.

How had he *known*?

She'd seen Ria do the same thing, instinctively reach for a spice that brought an ice leaping to life on the palate. It was a kind of alchemy. And totally frustrating when you couldn't do it yourself.

She needed Ria.

She needed Alexander.

No, Ria!

She checked the scales to see how much of the pepper

she'd used to the last gram, updated the recipe on her laptop, rounded it up and added the full amount to the churn. Then she checked her phone. No messages.

She started making the Earl Grey granita.

It wasn't one of their one-off recipes, but a standard they'd used before. Perfecting it was just a matter of timing to get the strength of the tea exactly right. No surprises, just concentration.

Alexander took a moment to gather his thoughts, concentrate on what he had to do in an attempt to shift the disturbing sense of losing himself.

It didn't help.

He flexed his hands, still tingling with the electricity of the touch of Sorrel Amery's fingers, palm against his. Cool, seductively soft, with contrastingly hot nails that exactly matched lips that were putting all kinds of thoughts into his head.

Dangerous thoughts.

It had been made very clear to him that his lifestyle and relationships were mutually exclusive. The era when women sat at home and waited while their men ventured into the unknown for months, years, had disappeared, along with the Victorians with whom Sorrel had compared him.

He'd made his choice and, while the passion for what he did burned bright, he'd live with it.

Alone.

He took a deep breath, then began to tackle the unpaid bills. When he'd placed the last of them in the out tray, he sat back and tried to piece together, from the fragments that had made it through the burble and static of a storm-disrupted uplink, exactly what Ria had said.

Sorrel wasn't the only one to immediately think the worst.

Her words had been distorted, broken, but the urgency of her plea for him to 'come now', the certainty that she'd been crying had been enough for him to abandon his search and fly home.

Finding the insolvency notice, tossed on the hall table amongst a muddle of bills, had been something of a relief. Financial problems he could deal with, but now it seemed that his 'Glad you're not here?' postcard, sent when he'd briefly touched civilisation a few weeks back, had triggered the downward spiral.

He felt for her, would clear up the mess, but he couldn't allow her to carry on like this. It wasn't fair on the people who relied on her. People like Sorrel Amery.

Unfortunately, in her case it was not just a simple matter of settling accounts and then shutting up shop. Despite her outrageously skimpy clothes, she appeared to have convinced sane men to hire her company. Sane men that he knew.

That took more than a short skirt and a 'do me' smile and in a burst of irritation he Googled Scoop!

There was more, he discovered. A lot more.

Scoop!'s website was uncluttered, elegant and professional. There were photographs of attractive girls and good-looking young men carrying trays that were a sleek update on the kind used by cinema usherettes and designed to carry a couple of dozen mini ice-cream cones or little glasses containing a mouthful of classic ice-cream desserts.

He clicked on one of the links—an ice-cream cone, what else?—and discovered Sorrel wearing a glamorous calf-length black lace cocktail dress with a neckline that displayed her figure to perfection. He'd seen something very similar in a photograph of his great-grandmother when she was a young woman.

Sorrel, unlike Great-grandma, was wearing the stop-me-and-buy-one smile that would have had him buying whatever she was selling.

Except that the smile wasn't for him. What she was selling was her business and that was all she'd been thinking about

today. While he'd been momentarily blown away by it, falling
into the waiting kiss and sufficiently distracted by it to let her
walk all over him, she hadn't wavered in her focus for a moment. She'd only ever had one thing on her mind—ice cream.

Which was the good news.

He told himself that the bad news was that he was stuck
with her. Unfortunately, he couldn't quite bring himself to
believe that. On the contrary, being stuck with her felt like a
very good place to be.

He'd definitely been out of circulation for too long, he decided. What he needed...

He forgot what he needed as he clicked through the links
to check out recent events and found himself looking at a photograph of a laughing bride about to take a mouthful of an ice
that exactly matched the heavily embroidered bodice of her
gown. He stared at it for a moment, a back-to-earth reality
check, before he clicked through the rest of the photographs.

A school football team celebrating a cup win, their traditional ice-cream cones containing black-and-white striped
ices to match their strip.

A company reception, the ices in the colours of the company logo.

He found the ice-cream van, too. Rosie, like the dress that
Sorrel was wearing, was a lovingly restored vintage and had
made appearances at any kind of event he could think of from
hen parties, birthday parties, weddings, even a funeral in the
last few months and she—someone—blogged about her very
busy life, including appearances in a television drama series
that was filmed locally.

He scrolled down until he found what he hadn't known he
was looking for. Sorrel Amery dressed as the Christmas ice-
cream fairy. The smile was, it seemed, not reserved for gullible men. She had her arms around a small, desperately sick

child, giving her a hug, making her laugh. And this time it brought a lump to his throat.

There was, apparently, a whole lot more to Sorrel Amery than long legs and lashes that fringed eyes the green and gold haze of a hazel hedge on an early spring morning.

But he'd already worked that out. She'd been concerned about her ice cream, her 'event' but, despite being badly let down, she'd shown concern for Ria, too. That displayed a depth of character that didn't quite match the skirt, the shoes or a kiss for a man she'd only set eyes on a minute before. A kiss that had left him breathless.

Apparently he was the one who was shallow here, leaping to conclusions, judging on appearances.

Sorrel hadn't fallen apart when her day had hit the skids. After a shaky start, she'd buckled down, dealt with the problems as they had been hurled at her and, in the process, convinced him to do something that went against every instinct.

That took a lot more than a straight-to-hell smile.

Sorrel was squeezing the juice from a pile of pink grapefruit when he returned to the kitchen. Not the most enjoyable job in the world, but she was putting her back into it.

'How long are you going to be?' he asked.

'As long as it takes,' she said. 'I'm going to have to make more than one batch of this so I'll be a while yet. As soon as I've got the syrup started, I'll pop down to the school to catch Nancy,' she said, checking her watch, before turning to look at him. 'You don't have to stay.' She favoured him with a wry smile. 'As you appear to have worked out for yourself, Ria gave me a key so that I can pick up stock out of hours.'

'That sounds about right.' Ria had a genius for making ice cream and if she'd been focused, seized the opportunities that clearly existed for someone with entrepreneurial flair, she could have been making serious money. He'd given her every chance, but it was obvious that she didn't have the temperament for it. As Sorrel Amery had discovered, she was like Scotch mist: impossible to pin down. 'I'm sorry she let you down.'

'It's not your fault and she didn't mean to. She's just, well, Ria.'

'Yes.' Infuriating, irresponsible, impossible to refuse anything... He'd berated Sorrel for handing over cash but he'd done a lot more than that over the years. Wanting to make up for her loss. His loss... 'I've got your lease.'

'That was quick.'

'It's a month's sub-let, hardly complicated.'

'Don't underestimate yourself.' She rubbed her arm against her cheek where a juice had splashed. 'You must be absolute dynamite when you've had a good night's sleep.'

'When I've had one, I'll let you know. In the meantime are you going to sign this?' he asked.

'I'll be right with you,' she said, squeezing the last of the grapefruit before peeling off the thin protective gloves.

She checked the date and signature on the original lease signed by Ria, then read through the sub-lease and the letter he'd written.

'You're my *sponsor*? What does that mean?'

'All our tenants are sponsored by a board member. You'll have to provide audited accounts and references before you'll be granted a full lease.'

'And will you sponsor me for that?'

'I won't be here.'

She flinched, as if struck. It was over in a moment and if he hadn't been looking at her quite so intently he'd have missed it. 'No, of course not,' she said. 'Um...this seems to be in order. Have you got a pen?'

'You're not going to read the actual lease?'

'Are you open to negotiation?' She glanced up, question-ingly.

'No,' he said, quickly, handing her his pen.

'Thought not.' She signed both copies of the sub-lease and gave him back one copy. 'You'll find my cheque pinned to the noticeboard.'

She'd been that confident?

'One month, Sorrel,' he repeated. 'Not a day…not an hour longer.'

CHAPTER SEVEN

I'd give up ice cream, but I'm no quitter.
—from Rosie's 'Little Book of Ice Cream'

NANCY WAS WAITING by the school gate for her little girl. Sorrel had expected her to be upset, to be looking worried, but, if the bright new streaks in her hair were anything to go by, her response to losing her job had been a trip to the hairdresser's. Far from depressed, she looked ready to party.

'Nancy…I've been leaving messages on your phone.'

She spun round. 'Oh, Sorrel…' She looked guilty rather than distraught. 'I was going to call you, but I've been a bit busy. Is there any news of Ria?'

'No, but I do have some good news for you. I've leased the ice-cream parlour for a month and if everything goes according to plan Knickerbocker Gloria is going to remain open.'

'Really? But Mr West said…'

'I know what Mr West said, but we've come to an agreement. I'll be employing you for the moment and once Ria comes back we'll sort everything out. In the meantime you can come in tomorrow and we'll carry on as usual.'

'Tomorrow?' Far from being thrilled that she still had a job, Nancy appeared panic-stricken.

'Is there a problem?'

'No… Yes…'

'Which is it?'

'The thing is, I can't, Sorrel. Not tomorrow.'

'Don't tell me you've got another job already? Not that you don't deserve one,' she added, quickly. 'Anyone would be lucky to have you.' Nancy was cheerful, hard-working and punctual, and it would explain the celebration hairdo. But no one was queueing up to offer part-time jobs to women at the moment.

Nancy pulled a face. 'Fat chance. Not that I've actually looked for one.'

'Well…' A day to get over the shock was understandable. And the hair thing might just have been a cheer-up treat.

'I did buy the local paper, but there was nothing in there. Then I saw an ad for a caravan.'

'A caravan?'

'By the coast. On one of those parks with pools and cycling and all sorts of great stuff for kids to do. Mr West had given me some money…I know it was supposed to see me through until I could get another job but when would I ever have that much cash again?'

Cash?

'You've booked a holiday?'

'It's just a week, but when I saw it, it came into my head, that thing that Ria is always saying. About seizing the fish?'

'What? Oh, *carpe diem*…' Seize the day. Or as Ria was fond of saying—when she'd taken off without warning to go to a rock concert or to dance around Stonehenge at the Solstice— 'Grab the fish when you can because life is uncertain and who knows when another of the slippery things will come along…'

'That's it. I realised this is what she meant. This is my fish. So I grabbed it.'

'But what about school? It's not half term, is it?'

'I checked with the head teacher,' Nancy replied, turning

from apologetic to defensive on a sixpence. 'She said a week by the sea would do Kerry more good than sitting in a stuffy classroom breathing in other kids' germs. She's had a really rough winter with her chest. I'm taking my mum, too,' she added. 'I don't know how I'd have managed without her.'

'I know…' Sorrel wanted to be happy for her. No, actually, she wanted to shake her for being so irresponsible about the money—*cash?*—but it wouldn't change anything. 'Well, I hope the sun shines non-stop and the three of you have a fabulous time.'

'I can come in next Friday. If you still want me?' she added, anxiously. Then, with a sudden attack of panic, 'I won't have to give Mr West his money back if I keep my job, will I?'

'What did he say when he gave it to you?'

'Just that it would keep me going for a while. He went to the bank to get it for me.'

'Did he?' She bit back a smile. It wasn't funny. Not at all. 'How kind of him.'

'He was lovely. So concerned. Not at all what I expected.'

'No.'

'Only what with the holiday, my hair and some new clothes for Kerry…'

Sorrel had to swallow, hard, before she could speak. 'Of course I want you, Nancy. And no, you won't have to repay Mr West. That was…' Since there was no money in the Knickerbocker Gloria account, that had to have been straight out of his pocket. And she'd yelled at him for not caring… 'That was a gift.'

'You're sure?'

'I'm certain. And in future you'll be working for me so we'll be starting afresh.' She opened her bag, took out her wallet and handed Nancy a banknote. 'Give this to Kerry from me. Ice-cream money.'

'That's too much.' Then, taking it, 'You're really kind.'

'Not at all.' Alexander West, on the other hand... 'This is work. Research. Tell her I want the full skinny on the competition. Flavours, toppings, colours, the whole works. With pictures.'

Nancy laughed. 'Right...' Then, her smile fading, 'Will you be all right? Who's going to run the parlour while I'm away?'

'That is not your problem,' Sorrel said, giving her a hug. 'I want you to spend the next week relaxing and having fun. I'll see you on Friday.'

'On the dot,' she said, turning away as the children came streaming out of school.

Sorrel stood and watched for a moment, a sharp little stab of pain of memory, loss, scything through her as Nancy scooped up her long-limbed daughter and swung her round.

Life is uncertain. Seize the day...

Alexander was making an inventory of the freezer contents when she returned. Needless to say he hadn't bothered with a white coat or hat, but he had fastened his hair back with an elastic band. It only served to emphasise his strong profile, good cheekbones, powerful neck.

'Why don't you go home and give your body a chance to catch up with the rest of you?' she said irritably as he stooped to check the bottom shelf and his jeans tightened over his thighs. He was just so...*male*! 'I'm not going to cheat you.'

He looked up, blue eyes fixing her with a sharp look. 'What's rattled your cage? Didn't you find Nancy?'

'Yes, I found her.'

Thanks to Alexander West and his unexpected generosity she now had an ice-cream parlour, but no one to run it. Nancy deserved a break, heaven alone knew, but the timing couldn't have been worse.

She washed her hands, put on the white coat, geeky hat and, aware that he was watching her, pointedly stretched a new pair of micro-thin gloves over her hands. She checked the syrup she'd made using the grapefruit juice, to make sure the sugar had dissolved, then poured half of it into one of the ice-cream makers. That done, she ripped the foil off a champagne bottle and attacked the wire.

Alexander closed the freezer door, put down the clipboard he was holding and, joining her at the workbench, held out his hand. 'Let me do that.'

'I can manage,' she said, continuing to twist the wire as if she were wringing his neck.

'I don't doubt it, but if you go at it like that you're going to break a nail.'

'Could you be any more patronising?' she asked, not bothering to look up.

'You're already having a seriously bad day and the last thing you need is to turn it into a disaster.'

She looked up, about to give him a piece of her mind, and saw that he was grinning. He'd been teasing her…

For a moment she was so surprised that she forgot to breathe. Then, without warning, she was spluttering, desperately trying to hold back an explosion of giggles. This was so not funny. Except that it was. And exactly what she needed. A good laugh…

'Bastard,' she said. 'A broken nail is not a disaster. But you're right, I don't have time to visit the nail bar.'

'That's better,' he said, taking the bottle from her and, while she struggled to get her giggles under control—stress-released, exactly like the bubbles in champagne, obviously—he dealt efficiently with the wire and, holding the cork firmly in one of those capable hands, twisted the bottle with the other so that they parted with no more than a gentle pop. None of that flashy fizz bang whoosh for Alexander West. 'I don't know what's upset you,' he said, setting the bottle on the work surface, 'but in that mood you're going to curdle the sorbet.'

'If I did it would be your fault.'

'Isn't everything?' he said, reaching for another bottle.

'Probably not,' she admitted, 'but I'm going to have to manage without Nancy and in this instance you are definitely to blame.'

That got his attention. 'Are you telling me that she's already found another job?'

'Oh, please. She never got as far as the job agency. You shouldn't have paid her off in, um, cash,' she said, demonstrating that he wasn't the only one who could lift one eyebrow at a time.

'I didn't have my cheque book with me.'

'Oh, I understand. I mean, who carries a cheque book these days?' she replied and he shifted his head an inch, acknowledging the hit. 'Unfortunately cash is a lot easier to spend.'

'She can't possibly have spent it all,' he protested.

'No?' Just how much had he given her? 'Not all, but a new hairdo, a holiday and some clothes for her little girl must have put a pretty big dent in it.'

He let slip a word that she wasn't meant to hear. 'I'm sorry, but that was supposed to tide her over until she found another job,' he said, exasperated. Not quite as laid back as he looked, then.

'You know that. I know that. Nancy…' She lifted her hand in a helpless gesture. 'I was so mad at her when she told me what she'd done that I wanted to shake her, but she hasn't had a break since her boyfriend decided that fatherhood was interfering with his lifestyle…' Her voice snagged in her throat. Women were so much at the mercy of their emotions. Of the men who took advantage of them and then walked away from their responsibilities.

Not her.

Not her…

'When I told her that I wanted her to come back to work, her first concern was whether she'd have to repay you.'

The same word and this time he didn't apologise.

'Of course she doesn't have to give it back. It was a redundancy payment from Ria's business.'

'From the business? You deducted tax and national insurance?' He began to peel the foil off a third bottle. 'Not that one. Not yet,' she said, reaching out to stop him, a jolt of warmth running through her hand as it closed over his.

His knuckles were hard beneath her palm, a little rough. Sun-bleached hair, gold against his sun-darkened skin, glittered on his wrist. She wanted to slide her fingers through it. Along his arm. Feel the hard muscle beneath the skin.

Alexander was staring at her fingers wrapped around his. They looked so pale against his, her nails painted to match her suit, so shockingly bright. Then he looked up and she saw what she was feeling reflected back at her, like a wave of heat. Undisguised, raw, shocking in its intensity.

Like her older sister, she had lived with the legacy of her mother's reputation, and had found it easy to resist temptation. Like her sister, all it took was a man with hot blue eyes to short-circuit her defences.

Speak...

She had to say something, break the spell, before she did something really stupid...

'I'm surprised...' Her mouth made the words, but no sound emerged and she swallowed, desperately. 'I'm surprised that if Ria had that much cash in her bank account she wasn't paying her bills.'

'Ria is owed money by a couple of restaurants.' He continued to hold her with just the power of his look. This is how it begins, she thought. This is the irresistible force that my mother felt... A phone began to ring from the depths of her handbag, shattering the tension. She ignored it. 'I'll get it back,' he said.

'Will you?' The spell broken, it was her turn to give him the disbelieving eye. 'Are you sure they didn't pay her cash on delivery?' she asked, carefully removing her fingers from his, taking the champagne bottle and setting it back on the work bench. 'For a discount?' Her shrug gave new meaning to the word 'minimalist'. 'She wouldn't last very long on the cash I gave her.'

'You're catching on.'

'Sadly not fast enough. If I'd had half a clue what kind of mess she was in…' She shook her head. 'I don't understand. She didn't seem bothered about a thing. The last time I saw her she seemed buoyed up. Excited.' She let it go. 'Unfortunately I now have another problem. Tomorrow is Friday, the weather men have promised us sunshine and we have no one to open up and serve the wonderful people of Maybridge with their favourite ice cream.'

'We?'

The 'we' she'd been referring to was Scoop!, but she was happy to include Alexander West since, for some reason that eluded her, he appeared to be taking the whole thing so personally.

'I'd do it myself,' she said, 'but, as you're aware, I have a major event tomorrow. I should be at Cranbrook right now putting everything into place.'

'I hope you're not suggesting that's my fault.'

'You're the one who gave Nancy the money to take off for a week,' she said, but with a smile, so that he'd know she wasn't mad at him for that. On the contrary, if she wasn't very careful, she could find herself liking him. Quite a lot. Despite the fact that he needed a haircut, didn't wear a suit and would rather hack his way through a mosquito-infested jungle than settle down and compete for the corner office like a proper grown-up.

Like Graeme, she reminded herself.

The man she'd picked out as her ideal husband. Mature, settled, everything that Alexander was not.

But then Alexander's smile crinkled up the corners of his eyes, tucked into a crease low in his cheek, emphasising the relaxed curve of his lower lip and for a moment she forgot to breathe.

'You do know how to use an ice-cream scoop?' she asked. 'You just press the handles together and…' He glanced warningly at her and she stopped. Whatever was the matter with her? 'It's got to be more fun than winding up a business.'

'You'll get no argument from me on that score,' he said.

'So, leave it until after the weekend. It seems a shame to spoil a sunny Friday doing a job that's custom made for a wet Monday morning.'

'Are you seriously asking me to run Knickerbocker Gloria tomorrow?'

Without thinking, she put a hand on his forearm. It was the simplest of gestures. Quiet appreciation of everything he was doing, no matter how unwillingly. 'I wish. Unfortunately you have to do the hygiene course before I can leave you in charge.'

'I do know how to wash my hands,' he said.

'I don't doubt it, but I'm afraid the Environmental Health Officer will require a certificate to prove it.'

He covered her hand with his own. 'It'll be tough, but I'll try and live with the disappointment.'

'I'm sure you'll survive. On the other hand…'

She paused.

'On the other hand what?' he asked.

'If you'll take Basil's place at Cranbrook tomorrow…' his eyes narrowed '…I'll ask Basil to run Knickerbocker Gloria until Nancy gets back.'

'Excuse me? Are you offering me a job?'

'I'll pay you the going rate.'

'That would be the minimum wage, I imagine.'

'A little more than that.'

'Don't tell me…all the ice cream I can eat.'

'At these prices?' She rolled her eyes. 'You've got to be kidding. I could offer you a discount on Rosie. If you'd like to hire her for a party?'

'How about next year's Christmas party at the hospice?'

'We already do that for cost, but if you'll come along and play Santa I could be persuaded to do it for nothing.'

'It's almost irresistible,' he said. The 'almost' suggested that he'd manage. To resist.

'Okay, I'll let you help me make the champagne sorbet. Final offer.'

'Without a hygiene certificate?' His smile was slow, meltingly sexy… 'Whatever would the Environmental Health Officer say about that?'

'When I say help, I was thinking about opening the champagne. For the second batch. Since you're so concerned about my nails.'

'Now who's being patronising?'

'I'll need a taster, too. Just in case Ria has been waving her wand over the mixture. After the great job you did with the cucumber ice cream, you're my go-to guy when it comes to magic.'

And that did it. His laugh, full-throated and deadly, rippled through her like a gentle breeze, stirring up all kinds of blush-making thoughts. It was such a good thing that he wasn't her type or she'd be in serious trouble.

'I should have thrown you out when I had the chance, Sorrel Amery.'

'It was never going to happen. I've got your measure, Alexander West.' It had taken her a while but, whatever his re-

lationship with Ria, her dreamy look was totally justified...
'Okay, here's my very final offer. All of the above plus dinner. I'll bet there's nothing but nut cutlets in Ria's fridge.' She
lifted one of her own eyebrows. 'Am I right? Or am I right?'

He shook his head. 'I thought...'

'What?' He didn't reply. He didn't have to. He'd made it
fairly plain what he'd thought. 'That I was all front and no
bottom?'

'On the contrary. When I saw you bending over that freezer
I thought you were all bottom and no front.' His gaze drifted
down to the open white coat, lingered momentarily on the
neckline of her chemise. 'Then you stood up and turned
around.'

She opened her mouth, closed it, tucked a non-existent
strand of hair behind her ear and then snatched her hand away,
remembering how gentle, how warm his fingers had been as
he'd done that.

'The champagne goes in the syrup...' She cleared her
throat. 'Whenever you're ready. Then you can turn it on and
set it to churn.'

'When do you want me to taste it?'

'When it's just starting to turn slushy.'

'What will you be doing?'

'Checking on progress at the business end of the event.
If you've no objections?' she said, leaving him to empty the
champagne into the syrup while she took a moment to call
her sister.

'Elle? Has the ice-cream bar gone to Cranbrook Park, yet?'

'All done. Sean stayed and set it up with Basil. Everything
is in place. How are you managing your end? You sound a
bit shaky.'

'Do I? Well, it's been a shaky sort of a day, but I'm getting there.'

'Any news of Ria?'

'Nothing, but I can't worry about her today.'

'Is it going to be a problem, Sorrel? What about that new chocolate ice for next week? Is that made?'

'No.'

'Terrific. I can't believe she'd do this to us!'

'I'll sort it,' she said, turning away so that Alexander wouldn't hear, 'if I have to go to Wales myself and find her.'

'Don't leave it too long. Wales is a lot bigger than you think.'

She called her uncle next and once he'd confirmed that everything was ready for tomorrow, she said, 'Basil, how do you and Grandma fancy running Ria's ice-cream parlour for a week starting tomorrow?'

'Serving proper old-fashioned ices? Banana splits? Chocolate nut sundaes with hot fudge sauce? Those fabulous Knickerbocker Glorias?'

'All of the above,' she said, laughing, mostly with relief that he sounded so enthusiastic. 'I'll organise a couple of students to come in and do the running around, but I want a really good show. Maybe you could create a bodacious sundae of your own?'

'Well, who could resist an offer like that? I'll have to check with Lally, of course, but you can count me in and I'm sure she'll be happy to help out, but what about the Jefferson event?'

'No problem.' She glanced at Alexander, who was standing over the churn watching the sorbet begin to chill. He really should be wearing a hat… 'I've got a volunteer ready and willing to stand in for you.'

'If you're referring to me, I did not volunteer for anything,' Alexander said, without turning around.

'Oh, and tell Gran there'll be one extra for supper, will you? I'm going to have to bribe him with steak and ale pie.'

CHAPTER EIGHT

Ice cream is like medicine; the secret is in the dose.
—from Rosie's 'Little Book of Ice Cream'

ALEXANDER, AS A matter of instinct, absorbed the sounds around him. In the rain forest it was a lifesaver. Here it was only the hum of the freezers, the whirr of the churn, the street sounds filtering in from the front of the shop. They were safe noises that he could filter out, allowing him to focus all his attention on Sorrel.

Her urgency, the slightest hesitation as she assured 'Elle' that she was coping, her determination as she turned her back on him, lowering her voice as she told her sister that she was prepared to go to Wales and find Ria. Good luck with that one. He registered the warmth in her voice as she spoke to someone called Basil, the hint of a giggle that made him want to smile.

Just being in the same room as her made him want to smile. Something he hadn't anticipated this morning when he'd discovered the extent of Ria's problems.

'Steak and ale pie?' he asked, since he had obviously been meant to hear that last part.

'Unless you're a vegetarian like Ria,' she said, 'in which case you can share Geli's tofu.'

'Who or what is Geli?'

'Angelica is my younger sister,' she said, joining him at

the business end of the kitchen to check the mix. 'The animal lover.'

'And Elle?'

'That's Elle for Lovage, Big Ears, although I'd advise you to stick to Elle when you meet her. She's my older sister.'

'The one with three little girls.'

'All under the age of five.'

'Good grief.'

'She makes it look easy and her husband is a fully engaged father,' she said. A shadow crossed her face so quickly that it would have been easy to miss. 'He's a dab hand with a nappy.'

'Good for him.'

'Yes…' Again that shadow, before she shook it off, looked up. 'Grandma is also called Lovage, but everyone calls her Lally.'

Sorrel, Angelica, Lovage, Basil; he was sensing a theme… 'Steak pie is absolutely fine with me, I just didn't expect to be having dinner with The Herbs.'

She pulled a face. '"And they shall eat the flesh in that night, roast with fire, and unleavened bread; and with bitter herbs they shall eat it."'

The face was meant to be comic, but he sensed that it masked some more complicated emotion and that if he probed a little, this supremely assured young woman might just fall apart. 'From the ease with which you trotted out the quotation, I'm sensing a lack of originality,' he said, sticking with the superficial. Ria was emotion enough for any man.

'A teacher who thought she was being particularly clever gave us that nickname when I was at primary school. My mother's name was Lavender.'

Was… He noted the past tense but didn't comment. He already knew more than enough about Sorrel Amery.

'The full set, then. So Fenny is presumably Fennel…'

'Just Fenny, actually. No one would call a little girl Fennel. But you've got the general idea. Her sisters are Tara and Marji.'

'Tarragon and marjoram? What would the baby have been called if she'd been a boy?'

'Henry.'

He grinned. 'Good King Henry?'

'You certainly know your herbs, although actually it's a family name on her father's side. Look, I'm sorry I can't offer you something more exciting by way of dinner, but I have a long day ahead of me tomorrow and you're not dressed for any restaurant I'd care to be seen in. It's The Herbs or nothing.' Then, as he shrugged, 'Do. Not. Do. That!' She turned away before he could respond and he glanced down at his shoulder where the gap in the seam had widened noticeably.

'I could take my T-shirt off if it bothers you so much,' he offered, barely able to suppress a grin.

'No!' she said, with more vehemence than entirely necessary. 'Forget the T-shirt. Here, taste…' She stopped the machine, took two plastic spoons from the pot, tasted the mixture, then handed the second spoon to him. 'What do you think?'

As he bent to dip into the mix his gaze intersected the point where the top of the silky thing she was wearing skimmed the top of her breasts and the last thing on his mind was sorbet.

He had absolutely no argument with her front. Or her rear…

'Well?' she demanded, when he took his time over filling the spoon, tasting the sorbet.

'It sort of sparkles on the tongue.'

'Right answer,' she said, briskly.

She was a little underdressed for the part but she was back in Businesswoman of the Year mode. It should have been off-putting. On his brief trips home his chosen partners were party girls who expected nothing more than a good time for as long as he was around.

Having kissed her, he thought perhaps he was missing out. Maybe he should widen his horizons…

'Is it sweet enough?' she asked. 'Bearing in mind that it's served with a touch of cassis in the bottom of the glass to add sweetness and colour, and berries threaded onto a cocktail stick.'

'I have to imagine all that?' He managed to imply that it was a foreign concept, but the truth was that his imagination was focused on other things. What her hair would look like loose about her shoulders, how it would feel, sliding against his skin… 'What kind of berries?'

'Raspberries and blueberries.'

'Pretty,' he said, putting the spoon in his mouth and sucking it clean. 'And—bearing in mind that I'm using my imagination regarding the liqueur and berries—there's nothing I'd add, although…'

'What?' she demanded after a long, thoughtful pause, clearly anticipating another 'eureka' moment involving some magic ingredient.

'I'm prepared to bet you a week's rent that it'll go long before the cucumber ice cream.'

'You really need to get over your hang-up about savoury ice cream,' she said crossly, switching the churn back on to freeze the sorbet. 'Look at the whole picture, the combination of tastes. Too much sweetness is cloying.'

'No danger of that with you, is there?' he said, leaning back against the work unit.

'Excuse me?'

'Sorrel—genus *Rumex*—used for medicinal and culinary purposes, is characterised by a bitter taste whereas…' Sorrel, torn between relief and annoyance that Alexander had teased her about the taste, paused in the act of dumping her spoon in the sink and turned to look at him '…*lovage*, pungent and

aromatic, is used in herbal love baths and *Angelica archan-
gelica…*' He paused. 'Is your sister angelic?'

'Only if you're an abandoned dog.' She gave him a sideways look. 'Of course, you're a botanist.'

'Only by accident. I'm actually a pharmacologist, but I spe-
cialise in medicinal plants.'

'Which include herbs.' She frowned. 'Ria is incredibly
knowledgeable about herbs. She makes a wonderful healing
cream using lavender.'

'I never leave home without it. We've a lot to learn from
the past as well as primitive societies.'

'And that's what you do?' she asked. 'Find the plants that
people have been using for centuries and bring them home to
find out what it is that makes them so special?'

'We're losing them at a frightening rate. Losing them before
we even know they exist. It's a race against time.'

'They're a lot more important than rare orchids, I guess.'

'More important,' he agreed, but then his face creased in
a broad grin. 'But nowhere near as erotic.'

'No one is going to miss you driving down the High Street in
that,' Alexander said a couple of hours later as Sorrel opened
the rear doors of her van so that he could load up the ices.

'That's the general idea,' she said, pausing momentarily
to admire Geli's artwork. The van was black, with Scoop!
drawn in loops of vanilla ice along each side and with a cel-
ebratory firework explosion of multicolour sprinkles, bursting
in a head-turning display from the exclamation point to splat-
ter the roof and the doors. It never failed to make her smile.
'And it means that you won't have any trouble following me,'
she said, going back inside to fetch more ices.

'Following you?' he asked, doing just that and reaching to
take big cooler containers she was carrying.

'Home…' They were both hanging on to the container and

much too close. 'For supper?' They were much too close. If she moved her fingers an inch their hands would be touching. If she touched him he would kiss her again…

She surrendered the load to him, turned and grabbed another container from the freezer, letting her face cool before following him to the van. He'd pushed his load deep inside and took hers and did the same with that.

'How are we doing?' he asked.

We. He was saying it now…

'Um… A couple more trips should do it.' He took the last load out to the van while she collected her bag, double checked that everything was switched off and set the alarm. 'Where are you parked?' she asked.

'I'm not. Ria took the car and I was too bushed to go home last night. I walked in.'

'You walked?' It was the best part of two miles from Ria's cottage and lesser mortals would have called a taxi.

'I needed to stretch my legs.'

'Obviously. No more than a gentle stroll in the park for a man who spends his days hacking through the jungle.' The tension that had gripped her throughout the day had eased now that everything was ready and she couldn't resist teasing him a little.

'I took the short cut along the towpath. A walk along the river at dawn is a good start to any day.'

'And no bats or mosquitoes to spoil the pleasure.' Only the newly hatched ducklings and cygnets being shepherded along the bank by their parents, the white lacy froth of cow parsley billowing over the path and blackbirds giving it their all.

'You have to walk along there in the evening if you want to see bats,' he said. 'Pipistrelles dipping and diving as they chase the insects.'

'Yes…' How long since she'd done that? Taken a run along the towpath in the morning before the day was properly awake.

Walked along it in the evening, not thinking, not planning, not doing anything but absorbing the scents, the sounds around her? 'We get them in the garden at dusk.' She smiled up at him. 'Maybe you'll get lucky this evening.'

'Will I?'

Alexander saw the touch of colour heat her cheeks as she realised what she'd said and he felt an answering heat low in his groin. For a moment neither of them moved, then Sorrel looked away, took her jacket from a hanger and slipped it over the silky top.

It should have made concentrating a whole lot easier but the image was imprinted on his mind and if she'd been wearing a sack he'd still see a tendril of escaped hair curling against her neck, her smooth shoulders, the silk clinging to her breasts.

That colour should have looked all wrong with her hair, but it was as spectacularly head-turning as the van. As spectacularly head-turning as the view of her legs as she slid behind the wheel.

When he didn't walk around and climb in beside her, she peered up at him. 'What's up, Doc? Don't tell me that you have a problem with women drivers?'

'If I said yes, would you let me drive?'

She grinned. 'What do you think?'

Women drivers in general didn't bother him. It was this woman driver in particular that had him breaking out in a sweat.

This morning he'd had a clear vision of what he was going to do. Close down the ice-cream parlour and, once that was done, go and find Ria, reassure her that everything was sorted. She could stay and spend the summer with her friends if she wanted, or come home. No worries.

He'd spend a few days dealing with the paperwork that piled up in his absence but, that done, he could return to Pantabalik and continue the search for an elusive plant he'd been hunting down for months. The one that the local people sang about, that he was beginning to think might simply be a myth. Or that they were deliberately hiding from him, afraid that he would steal it, robbing them of its power.

An hour or two in Sorrel's company had not just diverted him from his purpose, it had completely trashed it. Tired as he was, she had filled him with her scent, with colour, with her enthusiasm and distracted him with a straight-to-hell smile. Touched him with a look that had been filled with yearning for something lost. A memory that he had inadvertently stirred. He was good at that…

'Don't be such a macho grouch,' she said, laughing at his apparent reluctance to surrender himself to her unknown skill behind the wheel. 'I promise you, I didn't get my driving licence from the back of a cornflake packet.'

'Of course you didn't,' he replied. 'Everyone knows that women get their driving licences with coupons they save up from the top of soap-powder boxes.'

That provoked a snort of laughter. 'You are outrageous, Alexander West,' she said.

'Am I? What are you going to do about it?'

'Me?' She was looking up at him, her eyes dark and lustrous in the shade of the yard.

'There's only you and me here,' he said.

'Oh…' Her mouth pouted around the sound, invitingly soft. All he had to do was lean in and kiss her. Rekindle the fizz of heat that had continued to tingle through his veins all day. Take her up on the invitation to sit in a darkening garden with the scent of wallflowers filling the air, listening to the last lingering notes of a blackbird, watching for the first swooping flights of the bats.

How lucky could one man get?

Even from this distance he knew the answer. He didn't just want to kiss her. He wanted to draw her close, curl up somewhere quiet with her and go to sleep with the weight of her body against him. Wake up with her still there and see her looking at him just like that.

'One of these days, Alexander West, someone will take you seriously and you will be in such big trouble,' she said.

'You think?' He thought he was already in more trouble than he could handle. He would have happily fallen into bed with her, giving and receiving a few nights of no-commitment pleasure before kissing her goodbye and returning to work. But those sorts of relationships had rules. No eating with the family. Meeting grandparents, sisters. No getting involved.

Too late…

Time to bail before this got even more complicated and he did something really stupid that would end in a world of regret.

He dragged his hands over his face in a gesture of weariness that was not entirely faked. 'To tell you the truth, I'm already in trouble,' he said. 'The day has caught up with me and I'm going to fall asleep with my face in your grandmother's pie.'

Sorrel's shiver as she slid the key into the ignition, started the engine, had nothing to do with the fact that she'd been digging out her ices from the depths of Ria's freezers. It had everything to with the way that Alexander had been looking at her. A look that had bloomed, warm and low in her belly, and sent shivers of anticipation racing down her thighs. Shivers that every shred of sense told her were wrong, wrong, wrong.

So why did it feel so right?

'You have to eat,' she said, tugging on her seat belt, knowing that she was playing with fire, but unable to stop herself from striking the matches. 'A good meal is the least I owe you for rescuing my cucumber ice cream. And saving my nails.' She looked up and in that moment she knew exactly what he was doing. His reluctance had nothing to do with tiredness, or being driven by a woman. He was simply trying to find a polite way to excuse himself from the invitation that she'd thrown at him, and hadn't given him a chance to refuse.

That was her. Organising, a bit bossy... Well, she had to be if she wanted to get anything done. But this was different.

All day they'd been fencing with one another, touching close, kissing close. They weren't kids. They both understood how easy it would be to step over a line that should not, must not be crossed.

There was her life plan to consider and he probably had someone, somewhere waiting for him. He'd been kind, more helpful than she'd had any right to expect, but that was all. The kiss had meant nothing.

Ignoring a sharp little tug of disappointment, she said, 'On the other hand, gravy in the eyebrows is never a good look and, although I wouldn't have said anything, it's obvious that you're in desperate need of some beauty sleep.'

That provoked a wry smile. 'Thanks.'

'Don't mention it. Get in. I'll drop you at Ria's.'

'No need. It's out of your way and I need to loosen up. I'm not used to sitting at a desk all day.'

It wasn't—out of her way—but despite an almost over-whelming desire to drag him home, feed him and tuck him up beneath her duck-down duvet so that he could sleep the clock round in comfort, she could see that he meant it and she kept her mouth shut as he took a step back.

She should be grateful.

She wasn't the mother-earth type, brewing up herbs, making her own bread, creating out-of-this-world ices like Ria. Her world involved spreadsheets and cost accounting and a five-year plan that would put her name alongside the legendary local businesswomen Amaryllis Jones, Willow Armstrong, Veronica Kavanagh, who'd paved the way, who were her inspiration.

Besides, any man who travelled in places where there was

no mail service had to be capable of taking care of himself. Meanwhile, she had worlds to conquer, millions to make. Falling in lust with a man on the move was absolutely the last thing in the entire world she was ever going to do.

She shut the van door, lowered the window. 'You're quite sure? About the lift? I wouldn't want you passing out on the footpath.'

'Quite sure. Please give my apologies to your grandmother. I have no doubt that her pie will be wonderful, but I wouldn't do it justice.'

'Actually, when I said a good meal, I had my fingers crossed. Dinner with The Herbs tends to be a bit of a gamble. You may have had a lucky escape,' she said as she put the van into gear. 'Thanks for your help, today, Alexander. I really appreciate it and if you do hear from Ria will you ask her to call me?'

'Give me your number.' He took out his phone and programmed it into the memory, then nodded briefly, stepped back.

She sat for a moment, just looking at him until she realised that he was waiting for her to leave. He still had his phone in his hand and was probably going to call a taxi the minute she'd gone.

She gave him a little toot and eased out into the traffic. It was slow moving and Alexander passed her while she was waiting for the traffic lights to change.

He must have seen the van but he didn't slow or look around. She, on the other hand, watched him, a rather large lump in her throat, as he ate up the distance with a long, effortless stride. Then an impatient toot from behind warned her that the lights had changed and she was forced to turn with the one-way flow of traffic that would take her home.

It was only when she was pulling into the drive that the 'out of your way' penny dropped. He hadn't asked for Scoop!'s address, but it was on the sub-lease he'd prepared. He must have Googled Scoop! at some point during the day—she'd have done the same thing in his place—and, having discovered that the office was on the Haughton Manor estate, he'd assumed that she lived there, too.

'Wrong sister, Mr West,' she murmured, feeling just a touch smug. 'Not quite as smart as you think you are.'

Alexander headed for the river, stopping only to pick up fish and chips that he took to a bench beside the water, tossing more to the ducks than he ate himself. Wishing that he'd gone with Sorrel to share a family supper. It had been a very long time since he'd eaten home cooking.

Unfortunately, it hadn't been the pie that he'd wanted to taste.

Either the jet lag was worse than usual or he'd been in the jungle too long. Without a woman for too long. The heat had been there from the moment she'd turned around. A two-way glow that should have made it one easy step to the kind of brief fling that, when all the stars lined up, he indulged in on his flying trips home.

This morning the stars had appeared to be in perfect alignment but he'd known from the moment his lips touched hers that he'd made a mistake.

There had been nothing bold about her response to his kiss. Her lips had trembled beneath his tongue, her response a melting sigh, rather than a bold welcome. He'd known enough women to recognise that she was not the 'brief fling' type and brief was the only kind he could offer. A relationship conducted by satellite was never going to work. He'd tried it and had the returned engagement ring and Dear John letter to prove it.

He'd done his best to turn the kiss into an insult, hoping to send her running, but she'd had too much to lose and now his head was filled with the image of a body a man could lose himself in, a wayward curl that would not lie down, a soft giggle that made him hard just thinking about it.

He balled the paper, tossed it into a bin and set off along the towpath, walking the long day at a desk out of his bones. Walking off the restless energy of a libido on the rampage. Already missing her quick smile, her eagerness, her passion.

How many times today had he come close to repeating that kiss?

In his head he'd taken her on Ria's desk, against the freezer, his ice-cold lips against hot, hard nipples.

Maybe, he thought as he strode out in the gathering dusk, he'd misread the signals. Maybe if he went to Cranbrook Park tomorrow she'd repeat the invitation. Except that she didn't expect him to turn up to lend a hand at the Jefferson event. He'd seen the exact moment when she'd got the message, taken a mental step back and let him off the hook with her graceful exit.

A wise fish would ignore the siren voice whispering 'This one...' in his ear and swim away while he had the chance and, kicking his shoes off, he plunged into the river.

CHAPTER NINE

A little ice cream is like a love affair—a sweet pleasure that lifts the spirit.

—*from Rosie's 'Little Book of Ice Cream'*

SORREL TRANSFERRED THE ices to the chest freezer in the garage, shooed the dogs who rushed to meet her out into the garden and stepped into a kitchen filled with the smell of pastry burning.

'Hello, darling? Busy day?' Grandma asked as she turned from laying the kitchen table. 'Where's your friend?'

'Friend?' She checked the oven, turned down the temperature before the pie was incinerated and made a mental note to make an appointment to have her grandmother's eyes tested. 'Oh, you mean Alexander,' she said. 'He couldn't make it, Gran. He sends his apologies.'

'Alexander? Who's Alexander?'

'Graeme…' She jumped at the sound of his voice, turning guiltily as he appeared from the hall. Which was ridiculous. She had nothing to feel guilty about. She hadn't betrayed him. Only herself… 'I didn't see your car.'

'It was such a pleasant evening I decided to walk over from the rectory.'

'Really? It must be catching.' He frowned and she quickly

shook her head. 'Nothing. Sorry…I didn't expect to see you this evening. How is it going over there?'

'Slowly. Perfection can't be rushed.'

'I suppose not.' Was that why he was taking his time with her? Because she wasn't yet perfect?

'When I saw Basil in the village shop last week he asked if I'd take a look at his tax return so I thought I'd drop in and do it this evening. Kill two birds with one stone.'

'Oh? Who's the other bird?'

He frowned. 'You seem a little edgy, Sorrel.'

'Do I? It's been a difficult day.' Although not as difficult as it might have been thanks to Alexander. She forced a smile. 'It's very kind of you to help Basil.'

He shrugged. 'It's no trouble and I thought it would save you the bother of phoning me.'

'Oh, yes. Of course.' She'd put the opera so far in the back of her mind that she'd forgotten. 'I haven't had a chance to check the dates, yet.'

'Well, you can do that now. And you wanted to talk about the ice-cream parlour?'

'Isn't that three birds?' she said. And two of them appeared to be her. 'Bang, bang, bang.'

He should have laughed. Alexander would have laughed. Graeme merely looked confused.

She shook her head. 'Sorry. You're right. I do, Graeme. I'm going to ask Ria if she'd be prepared to go into partnership with me. I've had this absolutely brilliant idea—'

'Partnership? Are you mad?' he said, cutting her off before she could elaborate.

'Possibly. It's been a long day…'

'You're tired?'

Actually she wasn't tired, she was stimulated, elated, excited and didn't want to have cold water thrown over her idea.

'…and it's going to be a long day tomorrow. To be honest all I want to do right now is have a long soak and an early night.'

'Really? That's not like you,' he said, disapprovingly. Definitely not perfect… Clearly women who wanted to be world-class businesswomen didn't indulge themselves in a long soak in the bath when there were decisions to be made, ice-cream empires to conquer. But then most of them wouldn't have been on their feet all day producing the goods. And she did her best thinking in the bath. 'Very well. We'll have dinner tomorrow night. We can talk about it then.'

Uh-oh. She recognised that tone of voice. It was the 'must do better' voice. Talking about it meant talking her out of whatever silly idea she'd come up with.

'I'd prefer to leave it until the beginning of next week, Graeme. I'll have a better idea of the situation by then.'

'The situation seems clear enough…' He stepped back as the latest canine addition to the menagerie that had crept back into the kitchen began sniffing around his shoes.

'Midge! Out!' she said sharply and Midge, affronted, shook herself thoroughly, sending a cloud of white hair floating up to cling to Graeme's immaculate charcoal suit before she retreated to the step where she flopped down, blocking the door.

'Oh, for heaven's sake!' he exclaimed, irritably brushing at his legs. 'Your sister needs to grow up, Sorrel. This is your home, not an animal sanctuary.'

'I'm so sorry,' she said—she'd been apologising for Geli's waifs and strays for so long that it had become an automatic response—but honestly, any man with a particle of common sense would have changed into something casual before coming to call on a household with a large floating dog and cat population.

Alexander, in soft jeans and an old T-shirt, wouldn't have been twitchy about a few dog hairs. The thought crept, unbidden, into her head and she slapped it away. She was not going to compare them. Not to Graeme's disadvantage.

He might not be prepared to come and mix ice cream with her but he'd been there when she'd needed someone with experience to hold her hand as she'd launched Scoop! out of the shallow little pond of Rosie-based parties and into the deeper, more dangerous waters of major events.

While Elle and Geli had been happy to carry on as they were, he had understood her drive, her need to become a market leader, and encouraged her.

He'd been a guest lecturer on start-up finance during the final year of her degree, and she'd known, the minute he'd stepped up to the lectern, that he fulfilled everything she sought in a man.

Tall, slim, his hair cut by a famed London barber, his shirts and shoes handmade, his bespoke suits cut in classic English style, he passed the 'well groomed' and 'well dressed' test with a starred A.

His reputation as a financial wizard was already established, so that was his career sorted, and his property portfolio included a riverside apartment in London, a cottage in Cornwall to which he'd added the Georgian vicarage in Longbourne, when it came on the market.

'I'll find you a clothes brush,' she said, in an attempt to make up for her momentary irritation.

'Don't bother, it'll have to be cleaned.' And not looking up, said, 'Who's Alexander?'

'Alexander…?' Could he read her thoughts? For a woman who never blushed, her cheeks felt decidedly warm, but she had been bending over the oven. 'No one,' she said. 'Just a friend of Ria's.'

'One of those hippie types, no doubt.'

'Is Alexander a hippie? Does he wear beads?' Her grandmother smiled at some long-ago recollection. Then, with a little shake of her head, she said, 'I need some parsley.'

'I'll go and cut you some.' Welcoming the chance to step back from a loaded atmosphere, Sorrel took the scissors from the hook, stepped over Midge and cut some from the pot near the back door.

'Well?' Graeme asked, staying safely on the other side of the dog. 'Is he?'

'A hippie?' She made herself smile, less pleased with his slightly possessive tone than she should have been. Less pleased to see him than she should have been. She needed time to distance herself from Alexander, from the feelings he'd aroused, from some tantalising vision of what she was missing... 'Having only seen them in old news clips, Graeme, I have no idea,' she said. 'Perhaps you mean New Age?'

'You know what I mean.'

Yes, she was rather afraid she did. 'Well, he wasn't wearing flares, or flowers in his hair.' Edgy? She was balancing on the blade of the scissors slicing through the herbs... 'He's giving Ria a hand sorting out the Knickerbocker paperwork.'

'Typical. I can imagine how that's going.'

Why was he so annoyed? Did she have a big sign stamped on her forehead saying 'Kissed'...?

'Maybe, if you were nicer to her, she'd have called you,' she said, unable to resist winding him up a little.

He made a noise that in a less dignified man she would have described as a snort, but, instead of ignoring a business so small that it was beneath his notice, he seemed to take Ria's laissez-faire attitude to business, her lifestyle, as a personal affront.

'I'm sure he knows what he's doing,' she said, rinsing the parsley under the tap, giving it a shake and handing it to her grandmother. She didn't bother to tell Graeme that Alexander was a West. She didn't want to talk about him. At all. 'Not that it's any of our business.'

Something she'd been telling herself, without any noticeable effect, all day.

'If you're planning on getting involved, it's very much your business,' he pointed out. 'And if he's helping her, shouldn't Ria be the one feeding this man?'

'She's away.'

'Away? Where?'

'Dealing with a family emergency,' she said, without a blush. 'Without Alexander's co-operation tomorrow's event would have been a disaster, Graeme. Offering him a meal was the least I could do.'

'You shouldn't get involved.'

She didn't bother to point out that he was contradicting himself, merely said, 'I am involved. I need Ria. Scoop! needs Ria.'

'Why? Anyone can make ice cream. You did it yourself, today.' Something warned her not to tell him that Alexander had pitched in and helped with that, too. 'Don't even think of a partnership with that woman,' he warned. 'All you need is the equipment and you'll get that at a knock-down price in a creditor sale.'

Shocked, for a moment she couldn't think of a thing to say. But it was clear now why he'd been interested when she'd broached the idea of taking over the ice-cream parlour. He hadn't considered Ria's distress or Nancy and her little girl without an income. All he'd seen was a business opportunity. Simple economics. And clearly he expected her to feel the same way.

'I was using Ria's recipes,' she reminded him. 'They are her intellectual property.'

'For heaven's sake, Sorrel, it's not rocket science.'

'No...' It was magic.

'It's a little ahead of schedule but you have to seize opportunities when they come your way,' he continued.

'Carpe diem?' she suggested. The dangerous edge in her voice passed him by but her grandmother lifted her head and met her eye. 'The fish thing seems all the rage today.'

'You can take on one of the students who work for you,' he continued, ignoring her interjection. 'They'll all be looking for jobs when the school year finishes in a few weeks. You'll be able to pick and choose and they won't cost you more than the minimum wage.'

'Excuse me?'

'I know Ria is your friend but there's no room for sentiment in business, Sorrel. I can't tell you how much I disliked seeing you involved with someone who treated her business as little more than a game. She's run close to the brink of collapse a couple of times in the past. To be honest, I've been waiting for this.'

Clearly with some justification, but did he have to sound so satisfied that he had been proved right? So completely immune to the human cost?

'This is your moment to take control. You can pick up her local trade and expand it. You're building a strong brand image. You can capitalise on that.'

Apparently, while she'd been dealing with the practicalities, he'd been working out how to take advantage of the situation.

For her benefit, she reminded herself. He had no stake in this other than as her mentor. This was what she had always wanted. But not like this.

'I'm sure what you say makes perfect sense,' she said, 'and we'll talk about it when I can think straight, but right now if you don't mind I'm going to take the dogs for a run across the common before dinner.'

'I thought you were tired.'

'I am…' and she had a headache that was thumping in time to the whack of the knife through the herbs on the chopping block '…but I've been cooped up indoors most of the day and if I don't get some fresh air I won't sleep. I'd ask you to come with me,' she added, 'but you'd ruin your shoes.'

'Yes…' He appeared momentarily nonplussed at her dismissal, not because he wanted to come with her, but because he made the decisions. 'What about the twenty-fourth?' he asked.

She found her phone, ran through her calendar. 'I've got a wedding on the twenty-fifth…' A ready-made excuse.

'Oh, well, if it's going to be difficult—'

'No!' She'd invested years in this relationship. It was this, rather than some crazy fling with a man who would be gone in days, that she wanted. She wasn't going to fall out with Graeme over an ice-cream parlour. She'd produce a business plan. Maybe talk to someone else. Get another point of view from someone else who'd done this. 'I can manage.'

He nodded. 'I'll organise a car to bring you home.'

She knew he was conscious of being older than her, but there was taking things slowly and then there was the madness of kissing a man within moments of meeting him. She was not about to allow the fizzing heat that had erupted between her and Alexander West to derail her plans and sabotage the future she had mapped out so carefully.

'Is that necessary? I'll have to be in London the day after anyway.' She waited.

Say it…

Ask me to stay…

'Have you gone to brew that beer, Graeme?'

'Basil…' Graeme turned as her uncle came to see what was keeping him. 'Sorry…I was just having a word with Sorrel.'

'Oh, I didn't see you there, sweetheart. Take your time. I'll get the beers.'

'No, we're done here,' Graeme said. 'Call me when you've got time for a chat over the weekend, Sorrel. We'll sort things out then.'

Alexander had arranged an early meeting with Ria's accountant. The senior partner dealing with Knickerbocker Gloria had indeed been taken ill and his junior, overburdened and incapable of keeping Ria on a short rein, was more than happy to be relieved of the responsibility.

A line of credit to deal with any further bills had settled things at the bank. The ice-cream parlour was back in business, if only for a month. His next task was to put the accounts into some sort of order for Sorrel.

His assistant had emailed from Pantabalik to tell him that the rains had set in early and they were unable to travel any further upriver so it wasn't the worst time in the world to be away. He could follow up the research in the laboratory. Finish a paper he'd been working on for *Nature*. There were a dozen things to keep him busy while he was in England.

He arrived at Knickerbocker Gloria to find the door open and everything ready for what looked as if it was going to be a good day for the ice-cream business. A customer was already discussing her requirements with a distinguished-looking man in a straw boater, who was taking her through the flavours on offer, offering a taste of anything that caught her fancy, making suggestions, full of information about the quality of the ingredients.

He waited until she'd left with her purchase before introducing himself. 'Basil Amery? I'm Alexander West. This is very good of you.'

'No, dear boy. I'm enjoying myself, but what are you doing here? You should be at Cranbrook Park.'

'Should I?' Sorrel was expecting him? Last night, when she'd said goodbye, he'd been sure she understood. That he'd made it clear... So why did the day suddenly feel brighter? 'She was vague about the details.'

'Was she? That's not like her.'

'Probably my fault. Jet lag...' He left the explanation hanging as Basil turned and called back into the rear.

'Lally, my dear, what exactly did Sorrel say about Mr West?'

'Not much. I asked her if he was a hippie, but Graeme was there...' An elegant woman, probably in her sixties, but with the kind of bone structure that defied age, appeared from the rear. 'Are you Alexander?' she asked, with a smile he recognised.

'Alexander West,' he said, offering his hand over the counter. 'You must be Sorrel's grandmother. I can see the likeness.'

'No, it's Elle who features me. Sorrel is more like her mother, although where she gets that hair...' She shrugged as if to say that was anyone's guess.

'Maybe, but the smile is unmistakable.'

'Is it?' Rather than flattered, she looked bothered. 'Oh dear. It used to make my husband so cross...'

'You missed a jolly good pie last night,' Basil said, rescuing him.

'I'm sure,' he said, grabbing the lifeline. 'Unfortunately, I wouldn't have made very good company.'

'Better than Graeme. Such a fuss about a few dog hairs,' Lally said.

Graeme?

'It's a shame about the beads,' she continued, 'although they wouldn't do at Cranbrook Park. The boys are wearing white tennis shorts and polo shirts.' She eyed him up and down, then shook her head. 'Have you got a pair? Basil's won't fit you. Your waist is too narrow.'

'Only by an inch or two,' Basil protested.

'An inch is all it takes, darling,' she said. 'You can't hold a tray when you're hanging on to your trousers.' She turned that lambent smile on him and he could well see why a husband might get edgy… 'It's not a problem, Alexander. Jefferson's are supplying the clothes for the boys. Just pop in and tell them that you're part of the Scoop! team. They'll fix you up.'

Fortunately a customer arrived at that moment and, seizing the opportunity to escape, he said, 'I'll just pick up the books.'

Alexander hadn't come. Sorrel hadn't expected him. She didn't *want* him to come. He was a disrupting influence on her life.

He'd been quite clear that 'goodbye' had meant just that last night. Which was fine. It had been unreasonable of her to expect him to help out someone he didn't know. He'd done more than enough yesterday.

Her hand went to her lips and she snatched it away.

Everything was fine. She'd come prepared to fill the gap left by Basil herself. She'd even remembered to bring her camera to take photographs for the blog and, before the guests began to arrive, she lined up her well-drilled team of catering students from the local college in front of a mini Roman temple.

They were standing up close, girl, boy, girl, boy, half turned towards the camera, the girls' ice-cream coloured, full-skirted frocks billowing out to hide the rather pale legs of a couple of the young men who hadn't exposed them to the sun that year. Unfortunately, by the time she'd seen the problem it had been too late to send them to the local tanning salon for a quick spray, but once the lawn was filled with celebrities no one would be looking at their legs.

'Big smile, everyone,' she said, checking the screen to make sure she hadn't cut off any heads or feet.

She took half a dozen shots, but as she was about to tell them to relax a voice behind her said, 'Hold it. I'll have one of those.' She glanced round as one of the press photographers, prowling the grounds for atmosphere shots, came up behind her. 'You've got a good eye for a picture. Who are you?'

'Sorrel Amery from Scoop!' she said, checking his identity tag. 'We'll be serving the champagne tea. Who are you with, Tony?' she asked.

'*Celebrity.* Do you mind if I help myself to your pose?'

'Not if you promise to use the picture,' she said, slipping out one of the cards she had tucked at the back of her own identity badge and handing it to him, so that he would remember who they were.

'That's up to the picture editor, but a row of pretty girls always goes down well.' He glanced at the card. 'Ice cream?' He looked her up and down with a knowing grin. 'What flavour are you? Pistachio or mint?'

'Neither, she's cucumber.'

Her entire body leapt as a hand came to rest possessively on her shoulder.

'Alexander…' Calm, calm, calm… 'You're late. You very nearly missed your photo call.'

'I don't believe you actually mentioned a time.'

'Didn't I?' she asked, lifting her head to turn and look up at him, conscious only of the warmth from his fingers spiralling deep down inside her, spreading through her veins with a champagne tingle. 'You had my number. You could have called.'

'You could have called to remind me,' he replied.

'I assumed you'd slept through the alarm,' she said dismissively, making an effort to gather herself, step away from his drugging touch, 'and took pity on you.' Her brain responded. Her legs didn't. 'You must have been exhausted. It can take days to recover from jet lag.'

And finally he smiled. 'The beauty sleep didn't work, then?'

She looked at him. He was dressed for the part in a pair of immaculate and expensively cut tennis shorts and with a white polo shirt, every stitch firmly in place, clinging to his wide shoulders, but while the shadows, like bruises, that had lain beneath his eyes were gone, no one could call him beautiful. The underlying structure was good, high cheekbones, a firm jaw, but the nose had taken some knocks and in the bright sunlight she could see a series of fine raised scars on the side of his face, suggesting the lash of sharp, toxic leaves, that marred his cheek.

She wanted to run her fingers over them, smooth them away…

'I'm sure the photographer will give you a Photoshop glow if you ask him nicely,' she said, curling her fingers tightly into her palms as he turned to watch the girls giggling and putting on a show for the photographer.

'Thanks, but it would take a lot more than that to get me into your chorus line.'

'How much more?' The words were out of her mouth before she had the sense to close it.

He didn't look at her, but one corner of his mouth lifted in a lazy smile. 'I'll give it some thought,' he said, and her heart bounced like a tennis ball being tested by a champion about to serve for the match.

'Don't worry about it….' The 'don't' got stuck in her throat and the rest of the sentence never quite made it. She cleared her throat. 'An insect,' she said, flapping her hand as if to waft it away. His smile deepened. 'The thing about a chorus line is uniformity,' she struggled on. Everything about Alexander West was bigger, more dangerous than the students who hadn't quite made the leap from youth to manhood. 'You'd just make it look untidy.'

Worse, his maturity, his broad shoulders and muscular thighs, calves developed from walking miles in difficult terrain, would make them look ordinary. Not that she had seen how great his legs were when her heart had leapt. All it had taken to send it leaping about was the sound of his voice.

'I was going to get my hair cut, but I thought this was more urgent.'

He'd remembered what she'd said? Without thinking she put her hand on his arm. 'You'll do.'

'Will I?' And finally, he turned those hot blue eyes on her and she snatched back her hand as if burned before, not knowing what to do with it, she self-consciously tucked back the untameable curl. What was it about this man that made her act like a teenager? She hadn't done that since she was seventeen…

'Just this once. Hair above the collar next time,' she said, going for teasing, but not quite making it. 'I'm guessing, since you've come dressed for the part,' she said, giving him a casual once-over, just for the pleasure of looking at his legs, 'that you've been to the ice-cream parlour.'

'I called in for the books. I was going to put together the accounts.'

'And you got sandbagged by Basil and Lally?' So he was here out of guilt. But he *was* here… 'How are they doing?'

'Fine, although your grandmother seemed disappointed that I wasn't wearing beads.'

She smothered a groan, wondering what exactly her grandmother had said to him, thinking how good it would feel to hide her face in his chest, breathe him in, let his hand slide from her shoulder to her back. Well aware just how bad a move that would be.

'I'm sorry about that. She tends to say the first thing that comes into her head.'

'Someone must have put the thought there.' *Thank you, Graeme…* 'You have her smile.'

'Yes.' It used to get her grandmother into trouble, too… 'I

mentioned that you were a friend of Ria's. It's that New Age thing.'

Floaty, hand-dyed clothes, lots of exotic jewellery.

'It's okay. I got it. Have you heard from her?'

'Ria?' She shook her head. Why on earth would Ria call her when she could call him? 'I did find a postcard she sent me from Wales. It had a story on it. The legend of Myddfai.'

He grinned.

'I'm not pronouncing that right, am I?'

'Not even close. It's *muth* as in mother, *vi* as in violet.'

'Oka-a-ay…' Like she could ever have guessed. 'Would she go there, do you think?'

'Why? Are you planning to go and look for her?' he asked, not answering her question.

'I don't have much choice. She was going to develop a special chocolate and chilli ice cream for me.' He rolled his eyes. 'It's a special request for a local company who import tea, coffee, chocolate, spices. Adam Wavell? You might know him?'

'I might,' he admitted.

'He didn't insist on a tasting. We've worked for him before and he trusted me to deliver.'

'Did he know that Ria was involved?'

'It doesn't matter, does it? His contract was with me. Graeme is absolutely right. This is no way to run a business.'

CHAPTER TEN

Strength is the ability to open a tub of ice cream and eat just one spoonful.
—*from Rosie's 'Little Book of Ice Cream'*

'GRAEME?'

Sorrel blinked, slowly. He'd said that in exactly the same way as Graeme had said, *'Alexander?'*

'Graeme Laing,' she said. 'He's my financial advisor.'

His eyes searched her face, so close that she could see the starburst of navy blue that gave his eyes their ocean depths. The flecks of turquoise around the outer edge of his iris that lent a gemstone intensity to the colour. 'A little more than that, I think.'

'No…' The denial sprang to her lips, heat to her cheeks. It wasn't that she didn't blush, apparently, only that the occasion hadn't arisen before. But whereas Graeme had accepted her dismissal of Alexander as *'just a friend of Ria's'*, Alexander had instantly sensed that there was something more. 'I met him when he gave a lecture on business start-ups at university. I talked to him afterwards, asked his advice. He's been my mentor ever since.'

'He's not keen on dogs, I understand.'

Thank you, Gran…

'He's not wild about dog hair,' she admitted, 'but right now he's more concerned about Knickerbocker Gloria. He's advising me to let Ria go to the wall so that I can pick up the pieces for peanuts, then pay students the minimum wage to produce her ices. Pretty much what you suggested, in fact.'

'It's good advice,' he said, his hand slipping away from her shoulder. No-o-o… 'You should take it.'

'Probably,' she managed, through a throat thick with words, explanations that had no meaning. He had kissed her as if he had no ties, no bond. And she had responded as if Graeme did not exist because at the moment, when Alexander's lips had touched hers, he hadn't. 'He's helping me attain my ambition to be a millionaire by the time I'm twenty-five.'

'Then you should definitely take it.' He didn't look impressed by her ambition, but at least he hadn't laughed. 'How much time do you have left?'

'Only a couple of years,' she said. 'And while my business brain knows that Graeme is right, that you are right, given a choice between friendship and ambition, there's no contest. I'll take on Knickerbocker Gloria, but only if I can have Ria as a partner.'

He regarded her thoughtfully. 'Are you sure about that?'

'I'm not sure about anything, Alexander.' It wasn't just her business world that was falling apart; her life plan was crumbling to bits. 'The only thing I'm certain of right now is that you should have worn cricket whites instead of shorts. You're going to make my students look pasty.'

'I didn't realise it was an option but don't worry about it. No one is going to be noticing what those boys are wearing. Everyone will be looking at the girls.'

'All the men will be looking at the girls,' she said as he turned those blue eyes on the young women in their ribbon-trimmed ice-cream-coloured dresses. All the women would be looking at him. 'Would you like me to introduce you?' she asked. 'From left to right we have raspberry ripple, lemon cheesecake, Mexican vanilla, cherryberry sundae, coffee mocha cream and strawberry shortcake, also known as Lucy, Amika, Kylie, Poppy, Jane and Sienna.'

'Very pretty, but you were right about too much sweetness being cloying,' he said. 'I'll stick with cucumber surprise.'

'What's the surprise?'

He grinned down at her. 'Crisp and cool on the surface but with a soft centre and an unexpected kick of heat when you bite into it.'

That would be the heat burning in her cheeks. She had to put a stop to this before everything spun out of control. Now!

'You've got it totally wrong,' she declared. 'This dress is pistachio praline.'

He shook his head. 'Pistachio has more yellow in it and mint,' he continued, before she could argue, 'has more blue. That dress is definitely cucumber. Trust me. I'm a doctor.'

'Are you?' Stupid question. Of course he was. One who was intimately acquainted with plant life and undoubtedly knew what he was talking about. 'Then, I'm afraid, Dr West, you're a little over-qualified for this job,' she said, her own eyes straight ahead. 'You do know I wasn't expecting you to turn up today?'

'Basil thought you were.'

Basil thought nothing of the sort… 'I'm afraid you've been put upon by a past master in the art.'

'I don't do "put upon".'

Confused, she looked up at him. 'Then why are you here?'

'Because this mess is my fault, because you promised me home cooking—'

'Oh, right!' Well, that was all right, then. Guilt and food. She could handle that and she let out a shaky little breath, ignoring the tug of disappointment that flooded through her.

'And because I couldn't stay away.'

For a moment their gazes locked in a silent exchange that

surged through her body. Hot, powerful, unstoppable as a lava flow, it left her aching with hunger for this stranger who had erupted into her life.

She wanted this. Wanted him…

'Sorrel…' It took a moment for her to realise that Coffee Mocha Cream was speaking to her. 'I'm sorry to interrupt,' she said, blushing, not quite meeting her eye, 'but I think it's time we started.'

'Yes… Yes, of course…' She was too shaken to think of the girl's name. 'Jane…' It was Jane. 'Thank you.'

Alexander, as if knowing her legs were all over the place, casually took her arm as they headed up the hill towards the conservatory, supporting her until she could sit at one of the small tables, pull herself together. She had to write his name on a badge…

It didn't help that he sat in the chair beside her, his knee nudging against hers beneath the table, the froth of skirt between them no barrier to dizzying connection.

'Tell me what you need me to do,' he said, taking the pen from her useless fingers and doing it himself.

'I can't think…' He looked up, a slight frown creasing his forehead, and she realised that he was talking about the event. 'It would really help if you moved your knee…' Then, not quite able to believe she'd said that, 'I'm sorry…' She wasn't entirely sure what she was apologising for. Her inability to spell his name, or for being so completely lost in lust that she had forgotten the time, or for exposing her feelings so blatantly that she'd made Jane blush. 'I don't… It's not…'

'Breathe,' he murmured, fastening the badge to his shirt pocket. Shifting his knee a fraction, easing the pressure. Leaving only the heat… 'In and out. It helps—'

He was right. Remembering to breathe helped a lot. That, and the fact that he'd fastened the badge on upside down, proving that she wasn't the only one struggling to focus.

'What does Basil do, exactly?' he asked.

'Exactly?' That was it. Think about her uncle in his stripey blazer, making the women feel special… No, making *everyone* feel special. She took a breath. Okay. She could do this. 'Basil is a bit of a showman. He acts as a maître d' at this kind of event, keeping an eye on what's in demand and what isn't.' She managed a casual little shrug. 'Well, you've met him…'

'Yes,' he said, wryly. 'I'm sorry you've been lumbered with me.'

'I don't do "lumbered",' she said, and was rewarded with a smile. It should have made things worse, but, oddly, it didn't. It wasn't that kind of smile. It was a reassuring, we-can-handle-this smile. 'You'll be fine, Alexander.' More than fine… 'It's little and often with ices, as you can imagine. The trick is to keep the circulation going, make sure there's always something being offered and whisking away anything before it begins to lose its crispness.' She managed a wry smile of her own. 'There's nothing that ruins a celebrity's day like ice cream dripping on her designer dress.'

'Ria's accounts are beginning to look more attractive by the minute.'

'Too late,' she said. 'For the next two hours you are all mine.' And she concentrated on the exquisite tiled pattern of the conservatory floor so that he shouldn't see just how happy that made her.

'I imagine this is an equal opportunities company?'

'Of course it is,' she replied, then, realising that she'd missed something, she looked up. For a split second their eyes connected and the effect was like an electrical surge shorting her circuits. For a moment she couldn't move, couldn't speak…

'Two hours of your time… I'll tell you when,' he said, and this time his smile was definitely one of 'those' smiles.

Her hand flew to her heart to stop it hammering. 'I…um… Small quantities and speed of delivery is the answer, which is why I need so many waiters,' she managed to get out in a breathless rush. 'The students have all done this before so you shouldn't have any problems.'

'Why aren't they at class?' he asked.

Breathe... Air... 'I have a work-experience arrangement with the local college.' Better. Ordinary conversation would edge them out of the danger zone. Keep her focused on the job in hand. 'It's good for students doing catering and hotel management courses to have some hands-on experience to put on their CVs.'

'The money must come in handy, too.'

'Well, yes, and quite a few of them have found full-time jobs through me.' Yet another reason why it was so important that Scoop! didn't fail. 'I've organised a couple of them to help out in the ice-cream parlour, by the way. Basil is fit enough, but Gran can't work all day. Just in case you call in and wonder who they are.'

'Right... So where will you be?'

'I'll be in Wales. First stop Myddfai,' she said, and this time earned a grin for her pronunciation. 'Unless you can offer an alternative?'

'That will do as a starting point, but I was actually asking where you are going to be while I'm keeping the drips off the designer clothes?'

'Oh...' Stupid... 'Now that you're here, I can supervise the service. Did you know that you've got your badge on upside down.'

'Have I?'

'Oh, for goodness' sake. Everyone, this is Alexander,' she said, unhooking his badge and turning it around, fumbling a little as her fingers came into contact with the hard wall of his chest, the thump of his heart a slow counterpoint to her own racing pulse.

'Breathe slowly, Sorrel,' he murmured, putting his arm around her waist to steady her. As if that helped…

'Alexander…' she protested. He smelled so *good*. Nothing out of a bottle to obliterate the scent of fresh linen, warm skin… 'He's standing in for Basil today so if you have any problems he's your man.'

'I've got a problem,' one of the girls said, provoking a round of giggles.

'Raspberry ripple,' Sorrel muttered, under her breath, focusing on the badge. 'A bit of a handful.'

'That's what I thought about you.'

'That I was raspberry ripple? Or a bit of a handful?' He didn't answer and she looked up. 'Which?' she demanded.

'Both. But I was wrong. You're not raspberry.'

And remembering exactly when he'd last said 'not raspberry', she blushed again.

Alexander had no trouble keeping the flow of ices moving. The sorbet, mouth-wateringly pretty in chilled miniature cocktail glasses, didn't have time to melt before it was seized upon, while the mouth-sized bites of strawberry shortcake, little cups of Earl Grey granita, cucumber 'sandwiches' and all the other little teatime treats disappeared as fast as Sorrel and her team could dish them out.

Despite his teasing, he was seriously impressed and picked up some of her business cards to pass on to guests who asked him who was providing the ices.

Sorrel caught sight of Alexander from time to time, talking to guests, answering their questions, making sure that everyone was being served, keeping the flow of ices moving, just as Basil would have done. Making everyone feel special. With that smile, he was a natural.

He paused, occasionally, to exchange a word with guests,

pass on one of the cards she'd left on the counter of the ice-cream bar.

'I was wrong about the cucumber,' he admitted, at one point in the afternoon, when he brought back a few glasses that hadn't been returned to a tray.

'I told you I was pistachio,' she said.

'Not your dress, the ice cream,' he said. 'It's very popular, especially with the women.'

'Is that right? So are you ready to concede defeat?'

'That depends. Did we decide what your forfeit would be if you lose?'

'If I lose, I pay the full rent,' she reminded him, finding it easier to keep her head with the width of the ice-cream bar between them. 'Is there something you want, Alexander?'

His smile was slow, sexy and she was wrong about the ice-cream bar. It was nowhere wide enough.

'Ice cream?' she prompted.

'I have a special request for a tray of the Earl Grey granita for the ladies watching the tennis.'

'I suspect it's you rather than the ice they want.' Especially the junior royal who had been flirting with him whenever he came within eyelash-fluttering distance.

'Maybe you should send someone else.'

'And disappoint the paying customers? I don't think so,' she said, taking a tray of tiny cups and saucers out of a chiller drawer and piling in spoonfuls of granita, decorating each one with the thinnest curl of citrus peel, before adding a lemon tuile biscuit to each saucer with the speed of long practice.

'You've done that before.'

'Once or two thousand,' she said.

'They look very tempting.'

'Don't keep Lady Louise waiting,' she said, waving him away as she began scooping out the strawberry shortcake and lemon cheesecake into bite-sized biscuit cases. 'She won't be happy if her tea gets warm.'

'No, ma'am.'

When she allowed herself to look up again, he had been waylaid halfway across the lawn by a blonde weather-girl whose string of high-profile romances had ensured her permanent place on the covers of the lifestyle magazines. She leaned forward, offering a close-up of her generously enhanced cleavage, and, her hand on his arm, whispered something in Alexander's ear. He whispered back and she burst out laughing as she took a cup from the tray. Which was when the *Celebrity* photographer seized his moment.

Barring any outrageous incident, it seemed likely that her Earl Grey granita, bracketed by their favourite cover girl flirting with an unknown but attractive man, would make it onto the cover of next week's *Celebrity*.

She knew she should be ecstatic about that—it was more than she'd dared hope for—but, with Alexander still grinning as he headed for the tennis court, she couldn't bring herself to feel as happy about it as she ought to be.

'Fabulous, Sorrel,' Nick said, dropping by once everyone had gone. 'Thanks for a wonderful event.'

'It seemed to go well. We were lucky with the weather.'

'Well, I can't deny that helped. Alexander...' he said, turning, as Alexander handed her a couple of cups and a spoon that had been missed. 'I thought I saw you, earlier, but assumed I must be hallucinating.'

'I flew in a couple of days ago.'

'Actually, I was referring to the fact that you're moonlighting for Sorrel.'

'Blue moonlighting,' he said.

'As in "once in a blue moon",' Sorrel chipped in, seeing Nick's confusion.

Unsure what to make of that, he said, 'Well, thanks again, Sorrel. I'll be in touch very soon. It's my niece's eighteenth birthday in a couple of months and she's dropped heavy hints that she expects Rosie to put in an appearance at her party.'

'No problem. Just let me know when so that I can put it in the diary.'

'I'll phone you next week. Are you going to be around for long, Alexander?'

'A week or two.'

'Well, give me a call if you have time so that we can catch up.'

'Is there anything I can do?' he asked, when Nick had gone.

She shook her head. The students were a well-drilled team and everything was already cleaned down and packed away, ready to be picked up by Sean.

'You've been brilliant. I am very grateful. Truly.' She tucked the cups and spoons into their crates inside the ice-cream bar. 'Thanks for finding these. The staff are good at spotting stuff tucked away in the weirdest places, but it's always tougher keeping track when the event is outside.'

'I can imagine. So,' he said, 'what's the score? Who won?'

'Won?'

'What went first, the champagne sorbet or the cucumber ice cream?'

'Relax, the trust will get its rent. The sorbet had it by a country mile. We were down to the last scoop.'

'Perfectly judged, then. What happens to the ice-cream bar now?'

'Sean and Basil will come with a trailer and take it back to the estate.'

'Sean?' And there it was again. That same, slightly possessive tone.

'Sean McElroy. My brother-in-law,' she said, quickly, trying to ignore the little frisson of pleasure that rippled through her.

Bad, bad, bad...

'So he would be married to Elle? Father to Tara, Marji and Fenny?' He looked up as someone approached them. 'Yes?'

'I want a word with Miss Amery.'

'Graeme?' For the second time that day her heart catapulted around her chest at the sound of a voice. The first time it had soared. This time the reaction was confused. She should be delighted that he'd taken the trouble to come and see how the event had gone. Instead there was a jag of irritation that he should decide to choose today. 'What are you doing here?'

'Last night...' He made the smallest gesture with a well-manicured hand, a suggestion that what he had to say was for her ears only. That the help should take a hint and leave.

The 'help' ignored him and stayed put.

'Last night?' she repeated.

'You seemed keyed up, edgy, not at all yourself.'

'Really?' Why could that be? Because she'd invited herself into his bed and he'd chosen not to hear, perhaps? Because this was a relationship that he controlled and that until Alexander West had turned up, turned her on, she had been content to allow him to control. Because it was safe.

'When you didn't come back for dinner I was concerned.'

'Were you?' He hadn't been concerned enough to come looking for her. 'I walked along the river. I was safe enough with the dogs.'

'It wasn't your safety I was concerned about, but your state of mind,' he said. 'To be frank I'm concerned that you're going to do something foolish.'

'Why?' Alexander asked.

Graeme gave him a cold 'are you still here?' look, then said, 'We'll have tea here—'

'You've missed tea,' Alexander said. 'Shame. The cucumber sandwiches were a hit. Why do you think Sorrel would do something foolish?'

'Come along, Sorrel.' He used pretty much the same tone as she'd use to call one of the dogs to heel.

'Only I would have said that Sorrel Amery is one of the most level-headed women I know,' Alexander continued as if he hadn't spoken. 'I've seen her deal with a crisis with humour, compassion and a lot of hard work.'

'Who are you?' Graeme demanded.

'May I introduce Alexander West, Graeme? Ria's friend,' she added, quickly, before he said anything outrageous about her. 'He very kindly volunteered to step into Basil's shoes today. Alexander, Graeme Laing is my financial advisor.'

Graeme dismissed the introduction with an impatient don't-waste-my-time gesture. 'Where is Basil? Is he unwell? He was fit enough yesterday evening.'

'He's absolutely fine. He and Grandma are running the ice-cream parlour for me today.'

'For you?'

'I've rented it for a month while we sort things out. I need the facilities.'

'But that's ridiculous! Basil should be here.' He sighed. 'This is exactly what I was talking about. You've become emotionally involved, Sorrel. You have to distance yourself from that woman.'

'I can't do that. I need her.'

'Of course you don't! I've explained what you're going to do…' His voice was rising and, realising that he was attracting attention, he said, 'We need to talk this through in a quiet atmosphere. I'll go and reserve a table on the rose-garden terrace.'

Alexander said, 'Now, Sorrel.'

She reached back, a hand on his arm to indicate that she'd heard him. Sun-warmed, sinewy, it felt vital and alive beneath her palm, but she forced herself to focus on Graeme. She had to explain. She needed his support. Needed him to be onside.

'Distance is the last thing I want,' she said. 'I'm passionate about my business.' There had been plenty of time to think as she'd walked across the common, along the river bank in the gathering dusk with only the dogs for company. 'I want it to grow. Not just this,' she said, making a broad gesture with her free hand, taking in the sweeping parkland of Cranbrook Park, guests lingering after the event that had just taken place. 'I want everyone to be able to have a little piece of what we do. I want Ria to be my partner.'

She'd continued thinking as she'd soaked in the bath and then she'd spent a large part of the night drafting a proposal to put to Ria. A proposal that Graeme would understand—if he would just look beyond his prejudice and see the potential.

'I'm going to commission Geli to create a retro design for Knickerbocker Gloria and, once we've made it the best ice-cream parlour ever, I'm going to franchise it.'

'Franchise it? Are you mad? Have you any idea what that would entail?'

'I did some research last night and I got in touch with—'

'Sorrel.'

She turned to Alexander and he took her hand from his arm and held it in his. 'Now,' he said.

'Now?' she repeated, distractedly.

'I said I'd tell you when.' He raised one of those expressive eyebrows and the penny dropped. Two hours of her time. He'd tell her when.

Could he have chosen a worse time? Couldn't he see that this was important, not just for her, but for Ria?

She glared at him and then turned to Graeme. The contrast between the two men couldn't be more striking.

Graeme looked as if he'd just stepped out of an ad in the pages of one of those upmarket men's magazines. Whipcord slender, exquisitely tailored from head to toe, hair cut to within a millimetre, the faintest whiff of some fabulously expensive aftershave and an expression suggesting he'd sucked on a sour lemon.

Alexander had a touch of lipstick on his cheek, a smear of what looked like strawberry-shortcake ice on his sleeve and an expression that suggested he was enjoying himself.

Right at that moment she wanted to smack them both.

'I'm sorry to spoil your plans, Mr Laing,' Alexander said, before she could do anything, 'but Miss Amery and I have unfinished business and she's promised me a couple of hours of her time.'

'What business?' he demanded.

'Don't worry, Graeme,' she said, furious with him, furious with Alexander and, aware that she'd made a complete hash of it, not exactly thrilled with herself. 'It's got absolutely nothing to do with money.'

CHAPTER ELEVEN

Don't wreck the perfect ice-cream moment by feeling guilty.

—*Rosie's 'Little Book of Ice Cream'*

NEITHER OF THEM said a word until they reached the car park, where Sorrel snatched back her hand.

'Thanks for that.'

'He wasn't hearing you, Sorrel.'

'I know.' He wasn't hearing her about a lot of things. Or maybe she was the one not getting the message. 'It's my fault. I shouldn't have blurted it out like that, but it's what happens when you spend all night building castles in the air instead of getting a solid eight hours.' When you were distracted by desire and Mr Right was suddenly Mr Totally Wrong. 'My timing was off.'

'I may have caught him on a bad day, but Graeme Laing doesn't look like a castles-in-the-air kind of man to me. I doubt there's ever going to be a right time to sell him that deal.'

'No,' she said, leaping to his defence. 'You don't understand. He requires solid foundations, a business plan, a well-constructed spreadsheet to support the figures.' And even then he was hard to convince. She'd floated several carefully worked-out ideas by him during the last year and he'd shot them all down as 'impractical', or 'too soon'. She was never going to win him over by flinging something at him without careful preparation. 'He's not a man to talk things through on a walk by the river, throwing sticks for the dogs,' she added, more to herself than him.

'He's not a dog person, either?'

'What? Oh, no.' At least not excitable mongrels. If Graeme had a dog it would be as sleek and well groomed as he was. An Irish Setter, perhaps.

'Does he have any redeeming features?'

'He was brilliant when I was starting out, needed advice, support, finance. It's just…'

'He was talking to you as if you were a wilful child, Sorrel.'

'No… Maybe. A bit.' A lot. It was almost as if he didn't want her to expand. Wanted to keep her where she was. Which was ridiculous. He'd done so much to help her. 'I know how he thinks and I should have waited until I could lay out my business plan in a calm manner instead of jumping in with both feet.'

He looked down at her cream suede ballet pumps with flower trim. 'They are very pretty feet.'

She felt her face warm, her skin tingle. Two hours…

'Maybe he's not a foot man.' He looked up, his eyes full of questions.

She swallowed. 'The subject has never come up.' As far as she knew he'd never noticed her shoes. Floundering, she said, 'He's been very kind to me.' In company he was usually as courteous to service personnel as he was to captains of industry, but she couldn't help wondering how different his response to Alexander would have been if, instead of introducing him as Ria's friend, she'd introduced him as *'…one of the WPG Wests…'* 'He just has a bit of a blind spot about Ria. He can't see beyond the tie-dyed muslin and the bangles.'

'And her lack of responsibility when it comes to her accounts.'

'That, too. I keep hoping that he'll get it, see that the advantages outweigh the problems, but you can't change people can you?'

'No.'

'No,' she repeated.

She would always need security, while Ria would always seize the day, choosing life over her accounts, and Alexander would always need to be exploring some distant jungle, searching for new—old—ways to heal the sick. As for Graeme, he would always expect her to keep her emotions in check. Which hadn't been a problem until yesterday. Wasn't a problem...

'How did you get to Cranbrook?' she asked, not wanting to go there. 'Please tell me that you didn't walk.'

'Why?' he asked. 'Would you feel really guilty?'

'Why would I feel guilty? It's not that far from town. I was more concerned about the catastrophic effect that you, in shorts, would have had on road safety.'

He grinned. 'Are you suggesting that my legs are a traffic hazard, Miss Amery?'

'Lethal. The local Highways Department would have to put up warning signs if you were planning on staying for more than a few days.'

'Then it's a good job that I picked up my car this morning,' he said, sliding his hand into his pocket, producing a set of keys and unlocking the door of a muscular sports car. Apparently she wasn't the only one with a taste for nineteen-sixties vintage.

'This is yours?' she asked, running her hand over the sleek gunmetal grey curve of the Aston Martin's sun-warmed bonnet. 'It's beautiful.'

'It belonged to my father.' Catching the past tense, something in his voice that warned her that his father hadn't simply passed the car on when he'd bought a later model, she looked up. 'He died fourteen years ago,' he said, answering the un-asked question.

'I'm sorry.'

He shrugged. 'He had the kind of heart attack that most people survive. He'd treated himself to a yacht for his birthday and was having a little extra-marital offshore dalliance to celebrate. The woman involved, unsurprisingly, had hysterics. By the time she'd pulled herself together, worked out how the ship-to-shore radio worked and the coastguard had arrived, it was too late.'

'Alexander...' She was lost for words. 'How dreadful.'

'Are you referring to the fact that he was cheating or her inability to do CPR?'

'What? Neither!' She shook her head, not hearing the cynicism, only a world of hurt buried deep behind a careless shrug. 'Both. But to die so needlessly...'

'I have no doubt he gave St Peter hell,' he said, apparently unmoved by the tragedy. 'Particularly in view of the fact that he was the CEO of a company that manufactures the best-selling heart drugs on the market, a fact the newspapers made much of at the time.'

'I'm sure St Peter has heard it all before,' she said. 'I was more concerned about the effect on the woman with him. On your mother. On you.'

'I barely knew him. Or her. My parents split up when I was eight, at which point I was sent to boarding school.'

'But...'

'He was cheating on his fourth wife when he died. She couldn't have been surprised,' he said, 'since she'd hooked him the same way.'

He sounded distant, detached, and yet he'd kept his father's car, and she suspected the watch he wore had been his, too.

'My mother remarried within a year of the divorce,' he continued, anticipating her next question. 'Her second husband is a diplomat and they travel a lot. They were in South America the last time I heard from her.'

Distant, detached, uninvolved…

Her instinct was to throw her arms around him and give him a hug. It was what her mother would have done. It was what Ria would have done, but her own emotional response had been in lockdown for so long that she didn't know how to break through the body-language barrier he'd thrown up to ward off any expression of pity.

'You're a travelling family,' she said, because she had to say something.

'We travel. We were never a family.' He shook his head once, as if to clear away the memory. 'Shall we go?' he asked, abruptly. 'I'll follow you.'

'Right.'

Heart sinking at having triggered bad memories, she walked to her van. By the time she'd backed out he was waiting for her to take the lead, and as she drew alongside him she lowered the window and said, 'If we get separated by traffic head for Longbourne.'

She half expected him to suggest she'd be better off having tea with her financial advisor, which was undoubtedly true. The only danger Graeme represented was his prejudice against anything to do with Ria.

'Longbourne?' he repeated. No excuses, just surprise. 'I thought you lived at Haughton Manor.'

'That's my big sister. Sean is the estate manager and Scoop! rents an office in a converted stable block. No concessions for family,' she added. And then it hit her. 'It was your father who had the affair with Ria?'

He didn't answer. He didn't have to.

'That's why you feel responsible. Was she the woman on the boat?'

He shook his head. 'It happened years ago, when my parents

were still married. She was an intern working at WPG. Young, lovely, full of life, I imagine, and, from everything I know about him, exactly the kind of girl to catch my father's eye.'

'He married her?' she asked, stunned.

'Oh, no. She wasn't a keeper. She was too young, too innocent, too besotted to play that game.'

Too young for it to end well, obviously.

'What happened?'

'It's Ria's story. You'll have to ask her.' He was rescued by a toot from an impatient guest. 'We're blocking the car park.'

She glanced over her shoulder, raised a hand in apology and then said, 'If we get separated, drive straight through the village, past the common and you'll find Gable End about a hundred yards past the village pond on the right hand side.' Then, since the name was faded almost out of sight, 'White trim. Pink roses round the door.'

'It sounds idyllic,' he said, clearly wishing he'd let her walk away with Graeme.

'No comment, but if we're lucky there'll be a beer in the fridge.'

Alexander followed Sorrel through the posts of a gate that sagged drunkenly against the overgrown bushes crowding the entrance.

Blousy pink roses rambled over a porch, scattering petals like confetti and lending a certain fairy-tale quality to the scene, but closer inspection revealed that the paintwork was peeling on the pie-crust trim. If this really were a fairy tale, the faded sign on the gate would read *'Beware all ye who enter here...'*

He'd do well to heed it. He should never have gone to Cranbrook Park. Except that he'd enjoyed being part of it, enjoyed being with Sorrel, watching her at work, teasing her a little. Being close to her.

She'd touched something deep inside him, releasing memories, a private hurt that he'd locked away. There was only one other person he'd talked to so openly about his parents, but then Ria knew his history, shared his pain.

This was different. A dangerous pleasure.

Beware...

Sorrel drove around the side of the house. Here the modern world had touched what must have once been stables; the door opened electronically as she approached and she parked beside the ice-cream van he'd seen on the website. He pulled up in the yard and went to take a closer look.

'This is Rosie? She's in great condition.'

'She gets a lot of love and attention,' she said, smiling as she ran a hand over the van's bonnet, the same loving gesture with which she stroked the Aston's bonnet and then, as if aware that she was being sentimental, she looked back at him. 'You might think ice cream is frivolous, not worth bothering about, but her arrival changed our lives.'

'That sounds like quite a story,' he said, hoping to steer her away from what had happened to Ria.

'It is, but here's the deal. I'll tell you mine if you'll tell me yours.' She didn't wait for his answer but headed around the side of the house. 'Brace yourself.' As she opened the side gate, a dog hurled itself at them. Sorrel sidestepped. He caught the full force.

'Down, Midge! Geli, will you control this animal?'

'He's fine,' he said, folding himself up to make friends with a cross-breed whose appearance suggested a passionate encounter between a Border Collie and a poodle. The result was a shaggy coat that looked as if someone had tried—unsuccessfully—to give it a perm.

He ran his hand over the creature's head, then stood up. 'Come on, girl.'

Behind him, Sorrel muttered, 'Unbelievable,' as Midge trotted obediently at his side. By the time they reached the back door he had three dogs at his heels.

'Uh-oh…'

'Is there a problem?'

'If the sun's shining and the door is shut it means there's no one home,' she said, producing a key. Inside, the only sign of life was a cat curled up in an armchair in the corner of the kind of kitchen that had gone out of fashion half a century or more ago. The kind of kitchen that a family could live in although, in a house this size, it would once have been the domain of the domestic staff.

Sorrel peeled a note off the fridge door.

'"Gran too tired to cook so we've gone to the pub,"' she read, opening the fridge and handing him a beer. 'I should have thought.'

'You've had a lot on your mind,' he said, replacing the beer and taking a bottle of water. 'I'm driving.'

'You could always walk back along the towpath,' she suggested. 'It can't be more than three miles to Ria's. No distance at all for you.'

'Less, but I only flopped there last night because it was too late to do anything else. I have an apartment in the gothic pile,' he said, tipping up the bottle and draining half of it in one swallow. 'So, here's the sixty-four-thousand-dollar question.' Midge leaned against his leg, whining in ecstasy as he scratched her ear. 'Can you cook?'

'Cook?' she repeated, clearly anticipating that they would follow her family's example but, having snatched her from under the nose of a man who didn't have the courtesy to listen to her, he wasn't eager to share Sorrel with a pub full of people. He wanted her all to himself.

'I was promised home cooking,' he reminded her.

'Promises and piecrusts…' She looked up at him, half

serious, half teasing, and he wanted to kiss her so badly that it hurt.

Beware…

Too late.

It had been too late when he'd walked into Jefferson's and bought himself a pair of shorts and a polo shirt. When he'd agreed to sub-let Ria's ice cream parlour to her for a month. When he'd kissed her.

It had been too late from the moment she'd turned around and looked at him.

'Promises and piecrusts?'

'Made to be broken and in this instance it's for your own good,' she said, laughing now. 'Honestly.'

One of the other dogs sidled up and put his front paws on his foot, laid his head on his knee, nudging Midge out of the way, claiming his hand.

'You can't cook?'

'I can use a can opener and I have been known to burn the occasional slice of toast.' She shrugged. 'Sorry, but building a business has taken all my time.'

She was leaning back against a kitchen table big enough for a dozen people to sit around, cucumber fresh in the pale green dress that fitted closely to her figure then billowed out around her legs, masking the chilli that he knew lurked beneath that cool exterior. All he had to do was reach out, pull the pins holding up her hair and let it tumble about her shoulders…

'How about you? How do you survive in the jungle?' she asked.

Did that mean that she didn't want to take the easy option, either, but, like him, wanted to stay here? Just the two of them. Eat, talk, let this go wherever it would.

He took another long drink, felt the iced water slide down inside him. It didn't help.

'I don't starve,' he admitted. 'What have I got to work with?'

'Let's see.'

She stepped over a terrier, too old and arthritic to reach his hand. He leaned forward and stroked his head.

'Uh-oh.'

'That's the second time you've said that. I'm suspecting the worst.'

'Geli has been in London all week, Gran and Basil have been at KG all day. No one has been shopping.' She looked round the fridge door at him. 'Clearly it wasn't just Gran's tiredness that prompted an adjournment to the pub. What we have is a chunk of cheese, a carton of milk, a couple of cans of beer and some water.'

She turned to look up at him. Her skirt was brushing against his thigh, her lips were just inches away and for a moment neither of them moved. Then Midge nudged him, demanding his attention.

Sorrel looked away.

He caught his breath. He shouldn't be here. He shouldn't be doing this. A swift adjournment to the pub was the sensible move.

'The options are limited, but if your repertoire includes an omelette,' she said, holding up the cheese, 'I can handle the salad.'

'Great idea...' sensible clearly wasn't on the menu '...but we appear to be missing two of the vital ingredients. Eggs and salad.'

'Not a problem. Come with me.' She closed the door, picked up an old basket and headed down the garden, followed by the dogs. Once they were beyond the lilac, a daisy-strewn lawn opened up surrounded by perennial borders coming to life. Beyond it there was a well-maintained vegetable garden.

The walls were smothered with roses beginning to put out

buds, suggesting that it had once had a very different purpose, but what had once been flower beds were now filled with vegetables. One had a fine crop of early potatoes, onions and shallots were coming along apace and sticks were supporting newly planted peas and beans. On the other side of the wide, herb-lined grass path, rows of early salad leaves, spring onions, radishes and young carrots basked in a weed-free environment.

'Salad,' Sorrel said and, with a casual wave in the direction of a large chicken run sheltered beneath a blossom-smothered apple tree at the far end of the garden, 'Eggs.'

'You're into self-sufficiency?' he asked as half a dozen sleek brown hens and a cockerel paused in their endless scratching for worms to regard him with deep suspicion from the safety of a spacious enclosure.

'Not by design. There was a time when growing our own wasn't a lifestyle choice, it was a necessity. I hated it.' He caught a glimpse beneath the façade of the bright, confident woman who knew exactly what she wanted and took no prisoners to get it and saw a girl who'd had to dig potatoes if she wanted to eat. 'Fortunately, Gran has green fingers.'

'Not Basil?'

'Basil is the skeleton in our family cupboard. We didn't know he existed until five years ago when he and Rosie turned up on our doorstep.'

'That would be the long story?'

'Yes,' she said, 'it would.' She was smiling, so he guessed that part of it at least was a good one, but she didn't elaborate. 'When I was little this was a mass of flowers. The kind of magical country garden that you see in lifestyle magazines. It was even featured in the *County Chronicle*. Gran had help in those days and she held garden open days to raise money for charity.'

'What happened?'

'What always happens to this family, Alexander. A man happened.'

'I feel as if I should apologise, but I don't know what for.'

Sorrel shook her head and a curl escaped the neat twisted knot that lay against her neck. 'Gran's always been a bit fragile, emotionally. That's what a bad marriage can do to you. And then my mother died, leaving her with three girls to raise on her own. She was easy meat for the kind of man who preys on lonely widows who have been left well provided for. She needed someone to lean on...' She sighed. 'It wasn't just her. We all needed someone and he made the sun shine for us at a very dark time. He took us out for treats, bought us silly presents, made us laugh again. We all thought he was wonderful.'

'If your mother had just died, you were all vulnerable,' he said, wondering where her father had been while all this was happening. 'And likeability is the stock in trade of the con man.'

'I know...' She shook her head. 'He romanced us all, entranced us, but it was all a lie. He took everything we had and a lot more besides.'

'Did the police ever catch up with him?'

'We never reported it. What was the point? Gran had signed all the documents and I don't suppose for a moment he used his real name.'

'Even so.'

'I know. He probably went on and did the same thing to other women, but Elle was terrified that if the authorities knew how bad things were Geli and I would be taken into care.'

He looked around the garden. Hard times maybe, but what he was seeing here was survival. A glimpse of what had made Sorrel strong enough to stand her ground when he'd tried to drive her away. Strong enough to win business from hardheaded businessmen whose first reaction must have been much the same as his.

What he didn't understand was why she would need the approval of someone like Graeme Laing. The man had spoken to her as if she were a wilful child rather than an intelligent adult.

'You managed to keep the house,' he said. 'That's something.'

'He'd have taken that, too, leaving us out on the street without a backward look if he could have got hold of the deeds. He must have been digging for information when Elle helpfully explained that Grandad had left the house in a trust for his grandchildren. That it can't be sold until the youngest reaches the age of twenty-one.'

'Your grandfather didn't trust your grandmother?' He thought of Lally's distress when he'd mentioned her smile.

'They didn't have a good marriage and he spent most of his time working abroad, but I think it was my mother he was really worried about. She was a serial single mother; three babies by three different men, each of whom was just passing through. Elle believes that it was deliberate. She wanted children, a family, but she'd seen enough of her parents' marriage not to want a husband.'

'Are you saying that you don't know your father?'

'None of us do.' She lifted her shoulders in a careless shrug, as if it didn't matter. 'Probably a good thing.'

'Child support might have helped.'

'She didn't need it. Grandad looked after us, but I imagine he saw a time when some totally unsuitable man would realise the potential and, instead of planting his seed and moving on without a backward glance, would decide to stick around and make himself comfortable.'

'How on earth did you manage?' he asked. Trying to imagine how an old woman and three young girls had coped with a huge house they couldn't sell and no money.

'Elle held everything together. Held us all together, as a family. She sold anything of value to pay off the debts, the credit-card companies and, instead of going to college to study catering, she took a job as a waitress to pay the bills and make sure we didn't go hungry. She deserves every bit of happiness.'

And not just her sister... 'How old were you when your mother died, Sorrel?'

'Thirteen. Cancer, caught too late,' she said, matter-of-factly, but he saw a shadow cross her face like a passing cloud, and gone as quickly. 'It was just the four of us until Great-uncle Basil turned up.'

'He's your grandfather's brother?'

She nodded. 'He's been so good for Gran. She's a changed woman since he arrived.' And with that she summoned up a smile, putting the bad memories behind her. 'He does most of the hard work in the garden these days. The rescue chickens are a recent addition. Geli volunteers at the animal shelter and tends to bring home the overflow.'

'Rescue chickens? You're kidding.'

'They had scarcely a feather to bless themselves with when they arrived,' she said, opening the rear door and feeling inside the nest boxes for eggs.

'They don't seem very grateful,' he said, taking the basket, with its single egg.

'No.' She grinned. 'How do you feel about chicken soup?'

He laughed. 'Oh, right, I can see that happening,' he said, putting his arm around her and heading back towards the house. 'Don't worry. I'm going to be very generous and agree to eat in the pub.'

'Good decision. Just give me five minutes to change.'

'Not so fast,' he said, putting down the basket and keeping a firm hold on her waist, turning her so that she was facing him. 'There's one condition.'

'Oh?' She made a move to tuck the stray curl—the one with a mind of its own—behind her ear but he beat her to it, holding it there for a moment, feeling the flutter of her pulse as his thumb caressed her throat. 'What's that?'

'I get to choose the pub.'

Sorrel stopped breathing.

For a moment there she had remembered the mission. Security. Safety. To be in control of her destiny. To be the partner of a man who would be there always. Not like her grandfather who'd spent most of his life working abroad to avoid the woman he'd married. Not like her father, just passing through. Not like the man who'd reduced them to penury. But Alexander's hand was at her waist, his voice soft as lamb's fleece, wrapping her in a kind of warmth that she had never known.

His fingers were barely touching her cheek yet, from those tiny points of contact, energy flowed into her, firing a need, sensitising her skin so that she wanted to stretch like a cat, purr, rub against him, wrap herself around him.

They were standing so close that all she could see were his eyes. Everything else had faded away: the mad twittering of the sparrows in the hedge, the mingled scents of lilac and crushed grass, the agitated muttering of the hens. Her world had retracted to the ocean deep blue. She was sinking, going under... Sinking into a kiss that stole her breath, stole her mind, stole her body as his long fingers brushed against her shoulder and the pressure of his thumb against her nape sent ripples of pleasure down her spine.

He drew her closer so that she was pressed against him, breast to hip, sensuously plundering her mouth until her whole body was melting with a rush of intimacy, a need that stormed through her body, turning her legs to jelly. And then, when he was the only thing stopping her from melting into a little heap on the grass, he eased back to look down at her.

'Do you have a problem with that?'

Sorrel felt the world tilt. All the certainties she'd lived by fall away. She knew it was crazy, that next week, next month, he would be on the other side of the world, but some moments were to be seized.

Her mother had known that. Ria and Nancy knew it.

'No...' The word was thick on her tongue and even as she said it a dozen problems tumbled out of the woodwork, a hundred reasons why this had to be the worst idea in the world. Because he was asking for much more than her approval of his pub choice. 'Yes...'

Alexander had turned her world upside down, changing her from a woman in control of her life, her emotions, into someone who could forget everything when he touched her. He wouldn't take money, but he would steal her peace of mind, undermine the foundation on which she had built her future. Steal her heart. And then he'd leave...

With a supreme effort of will, she pulled away from him, putting air between them so that she could breathe, think. Sinking down onto the battered old bench by the back door before her legs gave way.

She took in big gulps of air, practically flinching as the noise rushed back in. Who knew that sparrows could be loud?

'I don't do this,' she said, her voice catching in her throat, and every cell in her body was screaming out to touch him. For him to touch her. 'I'm not like my mother,' she said, and it sounded like a betrayal.

'Aren't you? She knew what she wanted and went for it. Isn't that what you do?'

CHAPTER TWELVE

All I really need is love, but a little ice cream would do to be going on with.
—Rosie's 'Little Book of Ice Cream'

SORREL LOOKED UP at Alexander, her eyes huge. 'You don't understand.'

Actually, he did. She didn't do this, and neither did he. This was his cue to get up and walk away. He'd planned to drive to Wales this afternoon and find Ria, but he didn't even have to do that. She'd be back in her own good time and what happened next was Sorrel's decision, not his. Graeme Laing would be there to stop her doing anything foolish.

He could be on a flight back to Pantabalik tonight. It should be easy.

It had always been easy in the past. Even when he'd been engaged to Julia he couldn't wait to get back.

But he'd tried walking away from Sorrel and, as if he'd been held on a piece of bungee, he'd bounced straight back.

He didn't do this, but he took her hand and said, 'Ria had a baby.'

Her eyes widened. 'But she hasn't…' Then, 'She wouldn't…'

'No. My father gave her the money to dispose of his indiscretion but you're right, she didn't.'

'But…'

'She was very young and she was sure that once he saw the baby he'd want it. Ria is borderline bi-polar, high highs, low lows. She took her newborn son and presented him to his father on a dizzy high. You can imagine his reaction.'

'Poor Ria.'

'She collapsed with post-partum psychosis. Delusions, self-harm… The baby was taken from her, she was sectioned and by the time she had recovered her mother and my father had arranged for the baby to be adopted. She's been trying to find her son, my brother, ever since.'

'That's how you met?'

'I found letters from Ria, from her mother, amongst his papers after his death. He'd paid her mother…' He broke off.

'You contacted Ria? Hoping to find your brother?'

'Yes. If they'd gone through the proper channels I could have registered with them in case he ever decided to search for his mother. But it was a private arrangement and he was taken abroad.'

'Alexander…' Her hand tightened around his fingers. 'I'm so sorry. I wish she'd trusted me enough to tell me.'

He shook his head. 'It's not you, Sorrel. She never talks about it. She still feels terrible guilt.'

'She shouldn't.'

'No.'

'I'm glad she had you to support her.'

'I've done what I can. Tried to make amends. I hoped that the ice-cream parlour would give her a focus.'

'I can see why she loves you.'

'I love her, too. But not like this,' he said. 'Not like this.'

Like this?

Sorrel heard the words and Alexander was looking at her so intently that for a moment she thought he meant something more than the sexual frisson that had been burning up to the air between them from the moment they'd set eyes on each other.

Which was ridiculous. He hardly knew her.

She hardly knew him and yet her entire world was in turmoil. She couldn't think, could hardly breathe. It was as if she had been in suspended animation and had suddenly woken, seventeen again and on the brink of something amazing…

'Like this?'

Heart pounding, she reached out and touched his face where the lengthening shadows threw into relief the scars that ran in faint lines from his temple to his jaw, followed their path with her lips, trailing soft kisses across his cheek, the stubble of his beard sparking tiny flashes of electricity that buzzed through her. As her fingers reached his mouth she paused, raised her lashes and looked at him.

He would leave, she knew that, but he wouldn't steal her heart: she was giving it to him. Here, now, this was her day.

'Forget the pub,' she said. 'We can send out for pizza, but right now the only thing I want to eat is you.'

She didn't wait for his answer, but caught his lower lip between hers, sucking it in, wanting to taste him, devour him, and he responded like a starving man offered a feast.

The kiss consumed them both and she had no idea how they made it up the stairs to the small apartment she'd created for herself beneath the eaves.

She was only conscious of his mouth, of his hands beneath her skirts, on her thighs as, stumbling in their haste, she backed up the stairs, leading the way, pulling his shirt over his head, desperate to see, to touch what had until now been no more than tantalising glimpses of silken skin.

They tumbled through the door to her bedroom, breathless, laughing as he unzipped her dress. It fell in a whoosh of green cotton and white petticoats in a heap around her feet, leaving her standing in a white-and-green polka-dot bra, matching pants and lacy-topped hold-up stockings. And suddenly neither of them was laughing.

'Pretty...' His voice was thick as he stroked away the straps and kissed the curve between her neck and shoulder. She leaned towards him, wanting more, and he slipped the hook so that the bra joined her dress. His thumb lightly touched a painfully tight nipple, then his tongue, and she gasped as the shock of it went through her like a lightning rod. 'Very pretty...'

'Alex...' His name was a plea. She wanted to feel him, see him, possess him, and he lifted her, taking her down onto the bed with him.

Nothing she had done with a fumbling teen had prepared Sorrel for this. She wanted to throw herself on him, grab the moment, but the siren instinct, as old as Eve, was clamouring through her veins and, curbing the urgency to know, to be complete, she lowered her lips to a chest spattered with sun-gilded hair.

It tickled her lips as she feathered soft kisses down his throat, along his collarbones and he seized her as she flicked her tongue over his nipples.

'Wait!' she commanded. 'Wait...' She wanted him to remember this when he was on the other side of the world, up to his neck in jungle or lying on a hammock, or walking along a tropical beach. She wanted to remember this when that was all he was—a memory.

He grinned as he lay back, relaxed, arms stretched above his head, surrendering himself. 'Help yourself.'

Afterwards, he held her until she came back down, opened her eyes onto a new world.

'For a woman who's waited so long,' Alexander said, 'you were in an almighty hurry.'

Oh, God... 'I'm sorry. Did you...?'

'I most certainly did,' he said, before looping his arm

around her to pull her close, so that her head was on his shoulder and they were lying together, 'but next time we'll take it slower. Did you say something about pizza?'

Next time… She absorbed the fact that he wanted to do it again. 'I'm sorry about dinner.'

'I'm not. While you owe me dinner, I have a built-in excuse to keep coming back.'

'You don't need an excuse,' she said. 'You can come any time.'

He grinned. 'Give me a minute. I'm not a nineteen-year-old.'

'No, thank goodness.'

He glanced at her, but his call to the pizza parlour was answered at that moment and he concentrated on ordering, checking what she liked. Only when that was done did he turn to her and say, 'Okay. We have thirty minutes. Do you want to tell me about it?'

She shifted a limb that felt boneless. 'About what?'

'How you come to be the last twenty-three-year-old virgin in Maybridge. Possibly in the entire county.'

'I'm not…' He raised one of those expressive eyebrows. 'I wasn't…'

'No? I have to tell you that the nineteen-year-old who was there before me didn't make much of an impression.'

'No?' She thought about the very thorough job that Alexander had done and grinned. 'No.' Heady on the scent of fresh sweat, so relaxed that she was glued to the bed and aware that she was wearing a grin that would have put the Cheshire cat to shame, she said, 'Actually he was eighteen. I was seventeen and utterly besotted.'

'Lucky guy.'

'I thought I was the lucky one. He was captain of rugby, had a place at Oxford and he'd chosen to take me to the end-of-year school party.' She was going to be his summer girl, the envy of every other girl in village… 'He'd got hold of the key to the mat store at the back of the gym, but he was a little…over-eager. And then someone was tapping on the door. Apparently he wasn't the only one with ambitions that night.'

'Are you saying that your disappointment was so intense that you didn't bother again?'

'Well, it wasn't quite what the romance novels I'd read had led me to imagine. Awkward, fumbling…' Not like this. 'But I imagine, given the chance to practise, we'd have got our act together.'

'No doubt.' He smoothed a damp strand of hair from her forehead. 'Believe me, if that was your first effort, I can't wait to see what you'll do when you've hit your stride.'

She grinned. 'Maybe we should…' she danced her fingers down his breastbone '…you know. Just to make sure?'

He clamped his hand over hers, holding it where it was. 'You're not sure?'

She could feel his heart beating beneath her palm. A solid, regular thump that her own racing pulse picked up. It steadied.

There was going to be a next time. There was no rush…

'You can't blame a girl for trying,' she said, blowing on his sweat-slicked skin. 'I've got a lot of time to make up.'

'Quality, not quantity is the way to go. Tell me why it's taken you so long to try again?'

'Do I have to?'

She didn't want to talk about the past. She'd been clinging to it like a drowning woman to driftwood for too long but, having cast adrift so spectacularly, she wanted it done with. If she told Alexander now, she would never have to think about it again. Never look back, only forward.

'I've told you mine. It's your turn.'

She twitched her shoulders. What did it matter? She'd never told anyone, not even her sisters, carrying the shame of it inside her, but it had all happened so long ago.

'Okay. He'd been to a school disco, had a few swigs from a bottle of vodka someone had smuggled in and, when he got home a little bit high on mission accomplished, he did what any eighteen-year-old boy would do.'

He frowned, clearly not getting it.

'He dumped his clothes on the floor for his mother to pick up and wash.' Something Alexander wouldn't know about, she realised. 'I don't suppose you did that at boarding school.'

'No, but I'm getting the picture. She found a packet of condoms?'

'With one missing.'

'So? She had to assume that at his age he'd be trying to get into some girl's knickers. At least he was taking precautions.'

'It wasn't what he was doing, Alexander, it was who he was doing it with. My mother had three children by three different men. I look a lot like her except for my hair. She was blonde…'

'She assumed you were going to follow in her footsteps?'

'Three girls without a father to their name, living on their own with only a slightly dotty grandmother who'd lost all her money to a con man? Her imagination was working overtime and she packed him straight off to his uncle in America for the summer.'

'Presumably he could have said no.'

'Me, or the summer at Cape Cod with hundreds of girls who would fall for his…' she adopted an American accent '…"cute" English accent.' At the time it had felt like a knife being stuck into her heart, but it had happened a long time ago. 'Which would you have chosen at eighteen?' She didn't wait for his answer. 'I might have been besotted, Alexander, but I imagine he thought much the same as his mother.'

'Oh? And what was that?'

Exactly what his mother had thought was made very plain when she'd turned up at his house the following morning.

'That I was a little tart who'd lumber her son with an unwanted baby. Presumably that's why he'd picked me as his date in the first place. The tart bit…not the baby. He was smarter than that.'

'Well, you certainly showed them. Or did the rest of the village mothers keep their sons on leading strings?'

'If they did, it backfired. I could have dated any boy in the school that last year.' She could laugh about it now, but at the time she had just felt dirty… 'I finally understood why Elle didn't date.'

'She didn't?'

'We have a family song… *"Oh tell me, pretty maiden, are there any more at home like you? There are a few, kind sir, But simple girls, and proper too…"'* She began cheerfully enough, but then her voice faltered… 'Our family attracts scandal like wasps to a picnic.'

'There's more?'

She shrugged. 'Basil ran off with his girlfriend's brother and was written out of the family history by his father and brother. Grandma realised too late that she didn't like the man she was about to marry…'

'Too late? It isn't too late until the vows are made.' The teasing look vanished and there was an edge to his voice.

She raised her hand to his cheek, turned his face towards hers.

'Better to admit the mistake before the wedding,' she said.

For a moment he resisted, but then raised a wry smile. 'You're absolutely right. You can't expect a woman to hang around waiting for months, years…'

He will leave…

'What was her name?' she asked.

The only sound was that of a blackbird in the lilac below her window, the catch of her breath in her throat, and it seemed like for ever before he said, 'Julia. Her name was Julia. She decided my best man was a better bet.'

His bride and his best friend. Could it be any worse?

'I left him to help her organise the wedding. He was there with her, talking to the vicar, choosing the venue, doing all the stuff I should have been doing instead of being on the other side of the world playing Tarzan.'

'She said that?' she asked, shocked.

'She was angry. She had every right to be. And maybe a touch defensive.'

'More than a touch, I'd say. She must have known what you were doing when she agreed to marry you.'

'She'd assumed that I'd stop. Join the board of WPG. I may have given her that impression. I may even have believed it.' He glanced at her. 'It's not a mistake I'd make again.'

'No.'

Message received and understood.

He would leave…

A long peal on the door bell broke the tension.

'That will be the pizza,' he said.

'If we don't answer, maybe he'll leave it on the step.'

'And miss out on a tip?'

He leaned into a kiss, then flung his legs over the bed, pulled on his shorts and grabbed his wallet.

For a moment she lay back against the pillow, waiting for him to return. When he didn't immediately return, she panicked. This was all new to her. He was probably waiting for her to come down.

She scrambled out of bed, grabbed a handful of clothes and ran for the bathroom, splashed cold water on her face, scrambled into a T-shirt and jeans.

When she returned to the bedroom to drag a brush through her hair Alexander was lying back against the pillows. Shorts unbuttoned at the waist, ankles crossed, a pizza box unopened on his lap.

'You're overdressed,' he said.

'I get indigestion if I eat in bed,' she said. Which was true. 'And the dogs need walking.' Also true.

'And your family could come home any time.'

'I hadn't actually thought about that, but, yes, I don't suppose Gran will want to stay out late.'

'Okay.' He was on his feet in one fluid movement. 'We'll eat, we'll walk and then...' he said, taking her hand and heading for the stairs.

'And then?'

'And then,' he said, 'I'll kiss you goodnight and go home.' He glanced at her. 'We wouldn't want the neighbours gossiping.'

'Wouldn't we?'

Disappointment rippled through Sorrel. Right now she didn't care a hoot what the neighbours thought. Apparently she was a lot more like her mother than she'd realised.

She'd always thought she was strong, self-reliant, independent, but that wasn't true. She was still leaning on Graeme instead of stepping out on her own; allowing him to dictate the pace at which her business grew instead of relying on her instincts. Playing safe with both her heart and her head.

Even now, when she'd momentarily broken out of her shell, she'd ducked straight back inside it like a snail the minute she wasn't sure...

She should have been braver, waited until Alexander came back to her, and now he thought...

Actually, she didn't know what he thought.

'And we do have an early start in the morning,' he said.

'We do?'

'If we're going to Wales to hunt Ria down, we need to make an early start.'

'You're coming with me?'

'No, you're coming with me.' They had reached the bottom of the stairs and he stopped as if something had just occurred to him. 'Of course, if you came home with me tonight, it would save time in the morning.'

'Stay with you?' In his grace and favour apartment in the gothic mansion?

'My fridge is better stocked and we won't have to keep the noise down.' He lifted his shoulders in one of those barely perceptible shrugs. They lived up to their billing and she wanted to run her hands along them, her cheek, her mouth...

'What noise?'

'You're a bit of a screamer.'

'I'm not!'

He rolled his eyes.

She'd screamed? She caught a glimpse of herself in the hall mirror and discovered that she was grinning.

'Maybe your flat would be best,' she said. 'On the time front, I mean. You're a lot closer to the motorway.'

'Good point.'

'And you're right—if your car was parked outside all night it would be all over the village by breakfast time.'

'I thought you didn't care.'

'I don't,' she said, but Graeme should hear it from her, not from his cleaner. 'But then there's the screaming.'

'Why didn't your grandmother just return the ring and send your grandfather packing?'

'You know how it is,' Sorrel said, concentrating on scooping a string of cheese into her mouth.

They'd taken the pizza into the garden and were lying on the grass. She was aching in new places, a little sore, but it was a pleasant ache and she was feeling a deep down confidence that was entirely new.

Now Alexander had asked about her grandmother, prodding at an old wound, wanting to know why she'd gone ahead with the wedding, when his Julia had not.

'No, tell me.'

She stared up at the sky, following the movement of a small fluffy cloud, anything rather than look at him, knowing that he was thinking about another woman.

'The dress is made, the marquee has been ordered, the caterers booked,' she said. 'There are presents piling up in the dining room, crates of champagne in the cellar.' She turned to him then. 'It takes courage to defy expectations and call it off.'

'Would you have gone ahead with it?'

'I hope not, but it's a different world and Gran had defied her family to marry my grandfather.'

'Had she? He'd have been something of catch, I'd have thought.'

'Not for the granddaughter of the Earl of Melchester. She was a debutante, one of the "girls in pearls" destined for a title, or at least park gates. Great-grandpa Amery was trade.'

'Ouch.'

'As I said, it was a different world, but kicking over the traces is a bit of a family failing.' Was... Her generation had fought it. 'The choice was going home, admitting she was wrong and settling down with some chinless wonder, or going through with the wedding. Having made her stand, she chose to live with the consequences. There's no doubt he was as unhappy as she was.'

'With more reason. He had to live with his conscience. After what he'd done to Basil.'

'I imagine we were his penance. He lived with my mother's lifestyle choice, kept us under his roof, safe and cared for if not loved.'

He took another piece of pizza. 'Tell me about your mother.'

It was her turn to be silent for a while as she sifted through the jumble of memories, both good and bad. 'She refused to conform to anyone's rules but her own. She was pregnant at seventeen—the result of a fling with a showman from the fair that comes to the village on the first weekend in June. It set a pattern.' She glanced at him. 'We all have birthdays within ten days of each other.'

The corner of his smile lifted in a wry smile. 'She must have looked forward to summer.'

'Oh, she didn't lack interest during the rest of the year. She dyed her hair in brilliant streaks, wore amazing clothes and jewellery that she made herself and turned heads wherever she went.' The men looking hopeful, the women disapproving.

He glanced at her. 'But?'

She shook her head. The local women had no need to worry. 'When she wanted another baby, she chose someone who was just passing through.'

'A sperm donation? Only more fun than going to a clinic.'

'She was big on fun,' she said, then blushed.

He touched her cheek with his knuckles. 'There's nothing wrong with fun, Sorrel.'

'No…' She leaned against his hand for a moment. This wasn't just fun, but that was for her to know… 'She used to take us puddle-splashing in the rain,' she said, 'and when it snowed she'd take us up Badgers Hill and we'd all slide down on bin bags until we were worn out. Then we'd have tomato soup from a flask.' Her eyes filled with tears even as she was smiling at the memory.

'If if was so much fun, why are you crying?' he said, wiping a thumb over her cheekbone, cradling her cheek.

'Because I didn't tell her.' She looked up into those amazing blue eyes that seemed to see right through her. 'I should have told her…'

'You think she didn't know?'

'She sucked up every experience almost as if she knew she didn't have much time.' She swallowed down the lump in her throat. 'She loved life, lived every minute of it, seized every moment and didn't give a fig what anyone thought.'

'I envy you, Sorrel.'

'Well, that's new. No one has ever envied me for being the daughter of Lavender Amery before. There were times, when I was old enough to realise how different she was, that I waited until everyone had gone before I'd come out of school. When I hated her for being so different...' The words tumbled out. 'I wanted a mother who didn't stand out, who was part of the group at the school gate.' Who wasn't standing on her own. 'Just an ordinary mum.'

It was the first time she'd ever admitted that. Even to herself.

Alexander took her into his arms, then, held her. 'That's natural, Sorrel. Part of growing up. She'd understand.'

'I know she would. That only makes it worse.'

'We all feel a lingering guilt when someone dies. It's part of living.'

'It's hard to live down that kind of start in a small place like Longbourne.'

'No doubt, but it's not about your mother, is it?' The remains of the pizza were congealing in the box. 'It's about all the men in your life abandoning you.'

'No...' She swallowed. Yes... 'Maybe. I'd never thought of it like that.'

'So was the plan to become the Virgin Queen of ice cream?' he asked, lightly enough, but it felt as if her life, her future, her choices were suddenly being questioned.

'No. Of course not,' she protested. 'I was simply waiting for the perfect man to come along.'

'Oh, right.' He grinned. 'Well, I can see why it's been six years.'

'No...' She had to tell him. 'I found him a long time ago. Graeme ticked all the boxes.'

'Graeme Laing?' He didn't look particularly surprised.

'He's been my mentor since he gave a lecture at college and I stalked him for advice.'

'Classic. I bet he didn't know what had hit him.'

'Maybe not, but he was kind.' Flattered, amused even. 'We go to parties, business dinners, I get to mix with high-fliers…' Not that they ever treated her 'little' business as anything more than something amusing to keep the wife or girlfriend of someone as important as Graeme occupied when he had better things to do. But she watched them, listened to them, learned…

'Does he know that he's the chosen one?'

'We have—had—a kind of unspoken agreement that we'll get married eventually.'

'When you're grown up.'

'What is that supposed to mean?' she demanded, defending her choice.

'He's very nearly old enough to be your father, Sorrel, which is no doubt why he spoke to you as if you were a child.'

'I can see that it must look as I was searching for a father figure. Maybe I was. But he's not a man to kiss and run.'

'Not a man to do more than kiss, apparently. And he let me walk away with you without lifting a finger to stop me.'

'He didn't know—' She broke off. Of course he did. The sexual tension had been coming off them in waves when he'd turned up this afternoon. Jane had been embarrassed it was so obvious, and, while Graeme's emotional antenna was at half mast, he wasn't stupid.

If there had been a flicker of the heat that had consumed her from the moment she'd set eyes on Alexander, they would have fallen into bed a long time ago. She'd pushed him yesterday and he had grabbed Basil's interruption with both hands.

'You're right,' she admitted. 'He ticks all the boxes but one. There is no chemistry between us. No fizz.' It was as if he wanted her as his wife, but couldn't quite bring himself to make the commitment. Step over a line that he'd drawn when she was a new graduate and he was her mentor. And now it was too late. 'The moment I set eyes on you...' She tried to think of some way to describe how she'd felt. 'Did you ever have popping candy?'

'The stuff that explodes on your tongue?'

'Well, that's how I felt when I saw you. As if I had popping candy under my skin.'

CHAPTER THIRTEEN

A little ice cream is like a love affair—an occasional
sweet release that lightens the spirit.
—*from Rosie's 'Little Book of Ice Cream'*

SORREL HEARD THE words leaving her mouth and was aware
that she was totally exposed. Emotionally naked. She'd told
Alexander that she had her perfect man picked out, her life
sorted, but, overwhelmed by some primitive rush, the kind of
atavistic need that had driven women to destruction throughout the centuries, she'd thrown all that away because of him.

His hand was still on her cheek, his expression intense,
searching. 'I can't be your perfect man, Sorrel.'

'I know.' She lay back on the grass, looking up at a clear sky
that was more pink than blue. 'You don't tick a single box on
the perfect-man chart, especially not the big one.' She glanced
across at him. 'You're a wanderer. You'll leave in a few days
but I always knew that. I put myself in a straightjacket when
I was seventeen years old and thanks to you I've broken free.'

'That's a heck of a responsibility to lay on me.'

'No!' She put out her hand, reaching blindly for his. He
mustn't think that. He must never think that. 'I'm not Ria, Alexander. You don't ever have to feel responsible for me.' She
rolled onto her side to look at him, so that he could see her
face as she drew a cross over her heart and said, 'I promise

I will never call you across the world to rescue me. You've already done that.' She looked at him, golden and beautiful, propped on his elbow, a ripple of concern creasing his forehead, and she reached up to smooth it away. 'It's as if some great weight has been lifted from me and I feel light-headed, dizzy...'

He caught her hand.

'I want you to know that I don't do this. Get involved. I tried to walk away yesterday.'

'I know. We've both been caught up in something beyond our control. Don't analyse the life out of it. Just enjoy the moment.'

Then she laughed.

'What's so funny?'

'Nothing... It's just that my mother used to say that all the time. Enjoy the moment. This must have been how she felt.'

'And how does that make you feel?'

'Glad,' she said. 'I'm glad that she had moments like this.' She leaned into him, kissed him lightly on the lips. 'Thank you.' Then, because it was suddenly much too intense, 'I hope you're not still hungry, because the dogs have taken the rest of the pizza.'

'No problem.' He returned her kiss and this time he took his time about it. 'I'll cook something later.'

'Later'. Her new favourite word...

'What are we going to do now?' she asked.

'I'm going to get changed,' he said, standing up, pulling her with him, 'and we're going to take these unruly creatures for a walk.'

'Changed?'

'I didn't leave home like this. My jeans are in the car.'

By the time she'd picked up the chewed remains of the pizza box, thrown a few things into an overnight bag, Alexander was waiting for her in the kitchen. He was wearing worn-soft denims that clung to a taut backside, thighs that she now owned, but his T-shirt was black and holding together at the seams. A matter for regret rather than congratulation.

He took her bag, tossed it in the back of the car and then they set off across the common.

'Does it make you feel closer to him?' she asked. 'Your father's car.'

'Nothing would do that.'

'So why did you keep it?'

'You have got to be kidding. It's a classic. It appreciates in value.'

Maybe… 'It must have cost a fortune to insure for a seventeen-year-old to drive.'

'I couldn't get insurance until I was twenty-one,' he said, 'but let's face it, my father expected to be taking it out for the occasional spin himself until I was fifty. He had to make a new will when he remarried and I imagine the legacy was simply a response to a prompt from his solicitor regarding the disposal of his property.'

'What about the yacht? Did he leave that to you, as well?' Then, realising that probably wasn't the most tactful of questions, she added, 'All his best toys?'

His laughter shattered the intensity of the moment. 'No. It was too new to have been listed in his will so the widow got that, thank God.'

They walked the river bank until the bats were skimming the water, sharing confidences, talking about the things that mattered to them.

Sorrel shivered a little as he related some of his hairier adventures, and she came into the circle of his arm for comfort, afraid for him and the unknown dangers he faced. Animals, insects, poisonous plants and the guerrillas who'd held him hostage for nine months in the Darien Gap.

To distract her, he prompted her to tell him the 'long story' about Rosie and the Amery sisters' first adventures in the ice-cream business. Her ambitions, her ideas for Knickerbocker Gloria. The plan she'd wanted Graeme to listen to.

It was one of those perfect evenings that he'd take out and relive on the days when he was up to his neck in some muddy swamp.

It wasn't about the sex, although that had been a revelation. She had given herself totally, held nothing back, and neither had he. He couldn't remember the last time he'd been that open, that trusting…

He had no illusions. When he came back in six months or a year, or whenever, she wouldn't be sitting at home waiting for him. He wouldn't ask her to. He wanted her to have the life she deserved with a man who would be there for her. But for a couple of weeks she was his.

When they arrived back at the house everyone was home. He'd met Basil and Lally and they didn't seem surprised to see him with her, or that they were going to Wales to look for Ria.

Basil asked him how the Cranbrook Park event had gone. Her grandmother took his hand and smiled. Geli, her younger sister, gave him a very hard look, but since the dogs accepted him she was, apparently, prepared to give him the benefit of the doubt.

'You seem to have achieved universal approval,' Sorrel said as they drove across town.

'They were easier to impress than you.'

'I'm a tough businesswoman. You can't twist me around your little finger with your charm.'

'What did it take?'

'That would be telling,' she said, laughing. 'Your way with chilli powder, perhaps.'

The phone was ringing as they reached the door of his flat

and by the time he unlocked the door, the beep was sounding. 'Alexander? I've been ringing…'

He snatched up the receiver. 'Ria!'

'Oh, there you are. I've been trying to get hold of you for days. Have you changed your mobile?'

'I told you I'd lost my old one months ago,' he said, 'but I left you messages. Sorrel left you messages.'

'Oh… Sorry. I'm in the States and I disconnected my phone when I realised how expensive it was and bought a cheap model here.'

'In the States?' He switched the phone onto speaker, held out his hand to draw Sorrel closer. 'What on earth are you doing there?'

'I told you when I called you.'

'No, you didn't…' Or maybe she had. 'There was a hurricane, all that came through was that you needed me home immediately.'

'No, not home. I wanted you to meet me at San Francisco. When you didn't arrive I called again but your assistant said you'd already left. I've been worried—'

'What about the taxman?' he interrupted. 'The unpaid bills?'

'It's not important. I'll sort that out when I get home—'

'Not important? What about Sorrel?' he demanded, suddenly furious with her. 'Don't you ever think? She had a big event today and you left her high and dry to go swanning off to the States.'

'Today? No… That's next week… Isn't it?'

'Ria! What are you doing in America?'

'I… It's Michael,' she said. 'Michael's here. I've found my son, Alex. Your brother…' And then she burst into tears.

She'd found Michael? For a moment he couldn't speak and

Sorrel took the phone from him, talked quietly to Ria, made some notes, took a number.

'He'll call you back with his flight number, Ria.' There was a pause. 'No… It's fine, we managed. Really. But can you email me your recipe for the chocolate chilli ice cream…? That would be brilliant… No, take all the time you need. We'll talk when you get back.'

He heard her replace the receiver. Then she put her arms around him and held him while the tears poured down his cheeks, soaking into her shoulder.

She was smiling when he raised his head.

'I'm sorry…'

'No.' She put her fingers over his lips when he would have tried to explain. Kissed him. 'Ria has found your brother.'

'Look at me. I'm trembling. Suppose he doesn't want to know me?'

'He must have been looking for his family, Alexander.'

'Yes…'

She handed him the phone. 'Book your flight.' He held it for a moment, not wanting to leave her. 'Go on,' she urged.

He dialled the airline, then looked across at her. 'Seven forty-five tomorrow morning. You could come with me.'

'No. This is for you and Ria. And I've got things I have to do here. Chocolate ice cream to make. A franchise to launch if I'm going to be a millionaire by the time I'm twenty-five.' She tucked a strand of hair behind her ear. 'Let's just make the most of tonight.'

Alexander eased himself out of bed just before five the following morning, dressed quickly and picked up his overnight bag pausing only for one last look at Sorrel.

It was a mistake. Her dark chestnut hair was spread across the pillow, her lips slightly parted in what looked like a smile and he wanted to crawl back in bed with her. Be there when she woke…

She stirred as the driver of the taxi tooted from below. Her eyelids fluttered up and she said, 'Go or you'll miss your plane.'

'Sorrel…' He was across the room in a stride and he held her for a long moment, imprinting the feel of her arms around him, the taste of her lips, the scent of her hair in his memory.

There was a second, impatient, toot and she leaned back. 'Your brother is waiting for you.'

'Yes…' There was nothing else he could say. They both knew that he wouldn't 'see her soon'. He was going to fly west from San Francisco to Pantabalik, not because it made sense, but because if he returned he would have to say good-bye again.

Sorrel waited until the door closed, then she reached across to the empty side of the bed and pulled Alexander's pillow towards her, hugging it, breathing in his scent, reliving in her head the night they'd spent together.

They'd hardly slept. They'd talked, made love, got up to scramble eggs in the middle of the night before going back to bed just to hold one another. Be close.

She finally drifted off, waking with the sun streaming in at the window.

Alexander would be in the air by now, on his way to San Francisco to meet a brother he had never known before returning to the life he'd chosen. The life he loved.

She wanted to linger, stay in Alexander's apartment for a while, but that would be self-indulgent, foolish. She had seized the moment and now it was time to get on with her life, too.

She took clean underwear from the overnight bag she'd packed, had a quick shower and wrapped her hair in a towel while she got dressed. She found her jeans under the bed. Her

T-shirt had vanished without trace and instead of wearing the spare she'd packed, she picked up the one that Alexander had been wearing. Then she called a taxi and, torn between a smile and a tear, went home to get on with her life.

A new life. One without a prop.

She stopped the taxi outside the rectory and paid off the driver. Graeme saw her coming and was waiting at the door.

'Late night?' he asked, sarcastically.

'No,' she said. 'An early one.' And he was the one who blushed.

'Do you want to come in? I've just made coffee.'

'No…I have things to do. I just wanted you to know…' She swallowed. She didn't have to tell him. It was written all over her. She was wearing a man's T-shirt, for heaven's sake, coming home in a taxi in the middle of the morning. 'I hate opera.'

'You could just have said no,' he said.

'Yes, I could. I should have done that a long time ago. You've been a good friend, Graeme, and I'm grateful for everything you've done for me, but I need to move on with my life. And so do you.'

He sighed. 'You would have made the perfect wife. You're elegant, charming, intelligent…'

She put her hand on his arm to stop him. 'Perfect isn't the answer, Graeme.'

'No? What is?'

'If I knew the formula for love, Graeme, I would rule the world. All I can tell you is that it's kind of magic.' She kissed his cheek. 'Thanks for everything.' She was on the bottom step when she turned and looked back up at him. 'Did you know that Ria loves opera?'

'Ria? I'd have thought she was into happy-clappy folk music.'

'People never fail to surprise you. She's in San Francisco

right now, with her son, but she'll be home next week. It would be a shame to waste the ticket.'

There was a long queue in the arrivals hall to get through immigration and Alexander used the time to send Sorrel a text. 'Flight endless, queue at Immigration endless. I'd rather be making ice cream.'

Sorrel read his message and hugged the phone to her for a moment. She'd spoken to Ria that afternoon, explained her plans and said hello to a very emotional Michael.

He'd be waiting at the gate to meet his brother. Would they be alike? she wondered. Would they recognise one another on sight?

She took a deep breath then texted back, 'No, you wouldn't.'

He came right back with, 'I'm nervous.'

'He'll love you.' Who wouldn't? 'Now stop bothering me while I'm busy building an empire. I have ice cream to make. You have family to meet.' She resisted adding an x.

'Are you okay?' Basil asked, turning from the fridge where he was putting away the ices.

She sniffed. 'Fine. Bit of hay fever, that's all. How was business today?' she asked, before he could argue.

'Very good. Young Jane is a great find.'

'I know. I was thinking of asking her if she'd like to manage this place when her course is finished.'

'What about Nancy?'

'She doesn't have the business qualifications.'

'Maybe she should go back to school and get them. Knickerbocker Gloria could sponsor her.'

'You are unbelievable, do you know that?' She gave him a hug. 'The loveliest man in the world.'

'On the subject of lovely men,' he said, 'when will Alexander be back from the States?'

'He won't be.' She turned away, so that he wouldn't see how hard it was to say that. 'He needs to get back to work and he's travelling straight on to Pantabalik from San Francisco.'

'Well, I suppose that makes sense. But Graeme is history?' She nodded. 'Well, that's something, I suppose. I've nothing against him,' he added quickly. 'I'll miss his advice. But he was never right for you.'

'You didn't say anything.'

'Some things you have to find out for yourself.'

'I must be a slow learner.'

'No, my dear. There was no one else to show you how it should be.'

'No...' She swallowed, rather afraid that there would be no one else now she knew... 'I suggested he take Ria to the opera,' she said.

'Did you now?' He laughed. 'Well, she'll certainly shake the creases out of his pants. How's the ice cream coming along?'

'It's just about perfect,' she replied, offering him a taste.

'That'll put some heat into their tango.'

'You think? Great.' She swallowed. 'And I've created an ice of my own to go with it.' She took a fresh spoon and offered it to him. 'What do you think?' she asked, watching nervously as he tasted it.

'Oh, well, that's fun. What did you put in it?'

'Popping candy,' she said.

Alexander would have loved to find and name an orchid for Sorrel. But he wasn't in South America so he was searching the Internet for *Cattleya walkeriana 'Blue Moon'*, a rare, delicate pale blue orchid.

At the checkout he was asked if he wanted to add a message and typed, 'I saw this and thought of you.'

A few days later he received a text from her. 'Thanks, it's

beautiful. Did you know that the next blue moon is only a year away? Or three, depending on how you define it.'

'Let's go with the first definition,' he suggested. 'How's the new project?'

'Keeping me busy, but I thought of you and made this. I think it needs something else—any ideas?'

It was an ice-cream recipe. Milk, cream, sugar, popping candy...

He pulled out the T-shirt she'd been wearing that last night and held it to his face. Grass, fresh air, vanilla, strawberries swamped him with an overload of ideas, none of which he was prepared to commit to the Internet.

'Passion fruit.' He added a photograph of a huge blue butterfly sipping nectar from a tropical bloom and tapped, 'Just so you know that it's not all mosquitoes.'

Sorrel spread out Geli's designs for the new retro-look Knickerbocker Gloria.

'I've gone for classic nineteen-fifties Americana styling,' she said. 'Apparently they are the new "cool" in the States. I've sent you some URLs to check out.'

She'd put her phone on the table and when it pinged to alert her to an incoming message she stared at it.

'Do you want to get that?' Geli asked.

Yes, yes, yes... 'It will keep,' she said, turning to her laptop and clicking on the URL to a restored soda bar in New York.

'They do alcoholic ones?' she asked, a whole new level of opportunities opening up before her.

'When I was in Italy last year I was taken to an ice-cream parlour that served up seriously adults-only ices.'

'If we could get a licence, it would make a great venue for hen nights,' Elle chipped in.

'I'll check it out.'

Once they'd gone, Sorrel read Alexander's message,

touched a silky blue petal on her orchid, held his T-shirt to her face.

She made herself wait two days before she replied. 'The passion fruit was perfect. How do you do that, Postcard Man? Great butterfly, by the way. If the moths are that big, I'm amazed you have any clothes left.'

'Let's just say you wouldn't want to grow cabbages around here. How is the franchise plan coming along?'

'That's for the long term. We have to prove the idea first.' She attached Geli's design. 'This is the image we're going for.'

'Pure Norman Rockwell. Does Ria approve?'

'We're working on her.'

Alexander eased off his backpack, stretched his muscles, turned on his phone hoping for a message from Sorrel. After a long hard trek, it was like coming home to a kiss...

We're working on her?

'Who is we?' he dashed off and then wished he hadn't. He sounded jealous. Hell, he *was* jealous of anyone who was with her. Could Graeme be back on the scene?

He had to wait a day for her reply— 'Michael came back with her. He wants to see where he came from. Where you come from. He looks a lot like you, only less battered.'

'The knocks are collisions with experience. Michael is still a baby.'

'Keep away from experience, Alexander, it's bad for your health and rots your clothes. Any closer to finding the elusive plant?'

'Not yet, but there are plenty of others with potential. I sent a package of specimens back to the lab last week.'

'That's the way it goes. You're saving lives, I'm making ice cream.'

'Every life needs ice cream, Sorrel.'

And so it continued. Every day there was some small thing

to make him think, make him smile, make him wish he could reach out and gather her in. Feel her in his arms, smell her hair, her skin, taste her strawberry lips.

He sent her photographs of the plants he'd found, the shy people who lived in the forest, a shack by the river where he'd made camp, the perfect white postcard curve of beach he'd found when they'd been near the coast.

'Swam, baked a fish I caught over a fire and slept beneath the stars.' And, instead of simply enjoying the moment as he would have done before he met her, he longel for Sorrel to be there to share it with him.

'It looks blissful. I'm glad you had a few days out to rest. Michael has taken Ria back to the States for a couple of weeks, lucky thing. It's raining cats and dogs, here. Very bad for business.'

Julia had only ever asked when he was coming home. Ria only sent him messages when she needed something. Sorrel was different.

She asked what he was doing, what he'd found, how he'd managed to dry out his socks after heavy rain. He'd begun to rely on that moment at the end of a gruelling day when he could put his feet up and be with her for a moment.

'Make the most of it,' he suggested. 'Have a puddle-jumping moment.' He grinned as he hit send, hoping that she'd send a picture. He'd bet the farm that she wore pink wellington boots.

There was no picture. For the first time in weeks there was no message from Sorrel waiting for him at the end of the day.

It was some hang-up in cyberspace, he knew, and yet the absence of that moment of warmth, of connection when he returned to camp, left him feeling strangely empty. Cold despite the steamy heat…

As if a goose had walked over his grave.

He shook off the feeling. She was busy. KG was being refitted. She had a business to run, a million more important things to do than keep him amused, but sleep, normally not a problem, eluded him.

When there was no message the following day the cold intensified to a small freezing spot deep inside him and he began to imagine every kind of disaster.

He knew it was stupid.

She lived in a quiet village in the softest of English countryside. She wasn't going to find herself face-to-face with a poisonous snake in Longbourne. The only plant life that could cause her pain would be a brush with a stinging nettle and the mosquitoes weren't carrying malaria.

She could have had an accident, his subconscious prodded, refusing to be quieted. A multi-car pile-up in bad weather on the ring road—she'd said it had been raining hard.

She could be in a coma in Intensive Care and why would anyone bother to call him?

He tapped in, 'Missing your messages. Everything okay?' Then hesitated. He was overreacting. If anything was wrong, Ria would let him know.

Maybe.

But no one knew how he felt about her. He hadn't known himself until the possibility that she might not be waiting for him when he eventually turned up hit him like a hurricane.

No...

He deleted the message unsent; she was probably taking his advice and making the most of the moment. He hadn't asked her to wait for him. He hadn't wanted her to. He couldn't handle the burden of expectation that involved.

He hit the sack, but didn't sleep and after an hour he checked his inbox, again. Around one in the morning—lunchtime in Longbourne—he gave up and rang her mobile, telling himself that he just wanted to be sure that she was okay.

His call went straight to voicemail and the moment he heard her voice telling him she couldn't answer right now but if he left a message she'd get back to him, he knew he was kidding himself.

He wanted to hold her, wanted to be with her, wanted to talk to her but he was cut off, disconnected, out on a limb. It was the place he'd chosen to be. Right now, though, it felt as if someone were sawing through the branch and he were falling…

Sorrel had become part of his life and, without noticing, he'd begun to take it for granted that she always would be. The truth, hitting him up the side of the head, was that he couldn't imagine a day passing without her being a part of it. Couldn't imagine his life without her…

'Alex…' his research assistant, an Aussie PhD student taking a year out to do field work, stuck his head around the hut door '…one of the runners has brought in something you'll want to see.'

It was a leaf from the plant he'd been hunting for three years.

'It's not a myth,' he said, touching it briefly. Then he looked up. 'Go with him, Peter. You know what to do.'

'Me? This is your big moment, man!'

'It doesn't matter who brings it in,' he said, throwing his things into a bag. 'I'm going home.'

'You've got a family emergency?'

'Something like that.'

'I can't believe you've been working here on your own all weekend, Sorrel. What happened to the Jackson brothers?'

Sorrel eased her aching shoulder.

'Their mother was rushed into hospital on Thursday and I didn't have anything to do.' Well, apart from puddle-jumping and that was no fun on your own. 'It was just the finishing touches.'

She stood back, rubbing the inside of her arm against her

cheek. It came away smeared with paint and she used the hem of Alexander's T-shirt to wipe it off her face. She'd worn it on purpose, wanting the paint to obliterate his scent.

She had to stop sleeping with it tucked under her pillow so that she could catch his scent. Had to stop sending him little texts to keep him close and had to stop checking her inbox every five minutes, stop living for his replies.

She had to stop kidding herself that he would expect her to be waiting for him when he came back. He'd never even hinted that he wanted her to wait. On the contrary, he'd made it plain that he wasn't interested in that kind of commitment and his last message had been a wake up call.

He'd been honest with her. The least she could do was be honest with herself.

She had to live now, not for some fleeting blue moon moment that might never happen.

'Are you okay, Sorrel? You look…' Elle hesitated. 'Is there anything I can do?'

'I'm fine,' she said. 'I'll clean up here and then I'm going to walk home.'

'Walk?'

'It's stopped raining. The fresh air will blow away the cobwebs.'

'And the smell of paint.'

'That, too.'

It was late afternoon when the taxi pulled up in front of Gable End. Alexander paid the driver and walked around to the rear of the house. Midge greeted him with enthusiasm. The new puppy attacked his boots. He picked him up, tucked him under his arm and walked into the kitchen.

Basil looked round from the stove and beamed with pleasure. 'Alexander! Sorrel didn't say you were coming.'

'It was a spur-of-the-moment decision. Is she here?'

'She's been working at KG's all weekend. Putting the finishing touches.'

'On her own?'

'That's what she wanted. Elle just dropped in to see how she was doing. Apparently she's decided to walk home. Needs the fresh air.'

'I'll go and meet her.'

The river was running fast, the ducks had taken to the bank and there was no one out on the water. She had the towpath puddles to herself.

She hadn't replied to Alexander's suggestion she jump in one and he hadn't sent another. Clearly he'd felt obliged to respond to hers and she had been making more of it than it was.

It was time to send him one that would let him off the hook, one that conveyed the message that she'd enjoyed chatting with him long distance but she had to get on with the life she had, not the one that shimmered in the distance like a mirage.

It was time to seize the fish.

Alexander rounded the bend of the towpath and saw Sorrel standing fifty or so yards ahead, looking down at the phone in her hand.

She was wearing an old pair of paint-splattered jeans and one of his T-shirts, her hair was tied up in a scarf, there was a streak of blue paint on her cheek and he had never seen anything so beautiful in his life.

He'd covered half the ground between them before she looked up and in that second, before she could hide behind the killer smile, he knew that nothing could ever beat this. This coming home to the woman he loved, who loved him…

'Alexander…' Now the smile was back. 'What are you doing here?'

'I hated to think of you puddle-jumping on your own.'

'You flew halfway round the world to jump in a puddle?'

'No, I flew halfway round the world to jump in a puddle with you—'

And there it was again, a fleeting moment when she was emotionally naked and this time he didn't wait for her to fix the smile back in place but reached out for her, sliding his fingers through her hair, drawing her close to him.

'Don't you have puddles in Pantabalik?' There was a tremble in her voice that transmitted itself to his body. This was too important to get wrong.

'Not ones you'd want to jump in,' he said, 'at least not on your own because that's the other reason I flew home. To tell you that I love you, Sorrel. I'm home. If you'll have me.'

He kissed her then, before she could say anything. Telling her in the only way he knew that one day without hearing from her was too long. That he could not live without her.

When he raised his head, he saw that she was smiling, but it was a different kind of smile. Soft, tender, the smile of a woman fulfilled, the smile that had lived in his dreams.

'I won't leave,' he said.

She shook her head. 'I don't want to tie you to my side, Alexander. It's not the leaving that matters. All that matters is that you come back.'

Six months later Michael was Alexander's best man as he waited in a packed parish church for his bride.

Sorrel had been right. He'd had to leave, go back to Pantabalik, negotiate a settlement with the headman of the tribe for the harvesting of their precious plant. The texts had flown back and forth, full of warmth, fun, love, but he couldn't wait to get home.

Home.

He'd never had one before, but now there was Gable End, and the flat in the gothic mansion that Sorrel had filled with warmth and the house, perched high above the river bank, that they were building together.

He turned as the organist struck up, warning the congregation that the bride had arrived, and for a moment he could see nothing as his eyes misted over. Then she was there, her hand in his and looking up at him with the smile that no one but him ever saw as they seized the moment, the day, the life they had been given.

* * * * *